Bartleby & Co.

Bartleby & Co.

Enrique Vila-Matas

Translated from the Spanish by Jonathan Dunne

A NEW DIRECTIONS BOOK

Manufactured in the United States of America
New Directions Books are printed on acid-free paper.
First published in the U.K. by The Harvill Press, London, in 2004.
First published clothbound by New Directions in 2004.

Cover design by Semadar Megged

Library of Congress Cataloging-in-Publication Data
Vila-Matas, Enrique, 1948-
   [Bartleby y compania. English]
   Bartleby & Co. / Enrique Vila-Matas ; translated from the Spanish by Jonathan
   Dunne.
        p. cm.
   ISBN 0-8112-1591-1 (alk. paper)
   I. Dunne, Jonathan. II. Title.
   PQ6672.I37B3713 2004
   863'.64--dc22   2004016400

New Directions Books are published for James Laughlin
by New Directions Publishing Corporation,
80 Eighth Avenue, New York 10011

To Paula de Parma

The glory or the merit of certain men consists in writing well; that of others consists in not writing.

Jean de la Bruyère

TRANSLATOR'S NOTE

English quotations in the text have been restored to their original state (interesting here that the work of translation should have become the search for the original, which in many ways I think is what it is). I have translated foreign-language quotations myself, tying them in with existing translations.

Titles of works originally in English have been restored; titles of works in Spanish translated when their meaning is relevant to an understanding of the text; titles of works in other languages translated, where possible using accepted translations, when the author has himself translated them into Spanish in his text.

The curious reader will find a wealth of reading material – and one or two titles missing from library catalogues, "held in suspension in the history of the art of the No".

J.D.

I never had much luck with women. I have a pitiful hump, which I am resigned to. All my closest relatives are dead. I am a poor recluse working in a ghastly office. Apart from that, I am happy. Today most of all because, on this day 8 July 1999, I have begun this diary that is also going to be a book of footnotes commenting on an invisible text, which I hope will prove my reliability as a tracker of Bartlebys.

Twenty-five years ago, when I was very young, I published a short novel on the impossibility of love. Since then, on account of a trauma that I shall go into later, I had not written again, I stopped altogether, I became a Bartleby, and that is why I have been interested in them for some time.

We all know the Bartlebys, they are beings inhabited by a profound denial of the world. They are named after the scrivener Bartleby, a clerk in a story by Herman Melville, who has never been seen reading, not even a newspaper; who for long periods stands looking out at a pale window behind a folding screen, upon a brick wall in Wall Street; who never drinks beer, or tea and coffee, like other men; who has never been anywhere, living as he does in the office, spending even his Sundays there; who has never said who he is, or where he comes from, or whether he has any relatives in this world; who, when he is asked where he was born or given a job to do or asked to reveal something about himself, responds always by saying,

"I would prefer not to."

For some time now I have been investigating the frequent examples of Bartleby's syndrome in literature, for some time I have studied the illness, the disease, endemic to contemporary letters, the negative impulse or attraction towards nothingness that means that certain creators, while possessing a very demanding literary conscience (or perhaps precisely because of this), never manage to write: either they write one or two books and then stop altogether or, working on a project, seemingly without problems, one day they become literally paralysed for good.

The idea of investigating the literature of the No, that of Bartleby & Co., came about last Tuesday in the office when I thought I heard my boss's secretary say to somebody on the phone,

"Mr Bartleby is in a meeting."

I chuckled softly to myself. It is difficult to imagine Bartleby in a meeting with somebody, immersed, for example, in the heavy atmosphere of an assembly of directors. But it is not so difficult – it is what I propose to do in this diary or book of footnotes – to assemble a good number of Bartlebys, that is to say a good number of writers affected by the disease, the negative impulse.

Of course I heard "Bartleby" where I should have heard my boss's surname, which is very similar. But undoubtedly this mistake could not have been more propitious, since it made me strike out and decide, after twenty-five years of silence, finally to start writing again, writing about the last secrets of some of the most conspicuous cases of creators who gave up writing.

It is my intention, therefore, to make my way through the labyrinth of the No, down the roads of the most disquieting and attractive tendency of contemporary literature: a tendency in which is to be found the only path still open to genuine literary creation; a tendency that asks the question, "What is writing and where is it?" and that prowls around the impossibility of the same and tells the truth about the grave, but highly stimulating, prognosis of literature at the end of the millennium.

Only from the negative impulse, from the labyrinth of the No, can the writing of the future appear. But what will this literature be like? Not long ago a work colleague, somewhat maliciously, put this question to me.

"I don't know," I said. "If I knew, I'd write it myself."

I wonder if I can do this. I am convinced that only by tracking down the labyrinth of the No can the paths still open to the writing of the future appear. I wonder if I can evoke them. I shall write footnotes commenting on a text that is invisible, which does not mean it does not exist, since this phantom text could very well end up held in suspension in the literature of the next millennium.

1) Robert Walser knew that writing that one cannot write is also writing. Among the many minor positions that he held – bookshop assistant, lawyer's clerk, bank employee, worker in a factory that made sewing machines, and finally

major-domo of a castle in Silesia – Robert Walser would from time to time retire to Zurich, to the "Chamber of Writing for Unoccupied Persons" (the name could not be more Walserian, but it is genuine), and there, seated on an old stool, in the evening, in the pale light of an oil lamp, he would make use of his graceful handwriting to work as a copyist, to work as a "Bartleby".

Both his occupation as a copyist and Walser's whole existence remind us of the character in Melville's story, the scrivener who spent twenty-four hours a day in the office. Roberto Calasso, referring to Walser and Bartleby, has remarked that in such beings who have the appearance of ordinary and discreet men there is, however, to be found an alarming tendency to negate the world. All the more radical the less it is observed, the blast of destruction is frequently ignored by people who consider the Bartlebys to be grey, good-natured beings. "For many, Walser, the author of *Jakob von Gunten*," writes Calasso, "is still a familiar figure and it is possible to read even that his nihilism is middle class and good-natured like the Swiss. And yet he is a remote character, a parallel path of nature, an almost indiscernible knife-edge. Walser's obedience, like Bartleby's disobedience, presupposes a total break [. . .]. They copy, they transcribe texts that pass through them like a transparent sheet. They make no special pronouncements, no attempt to modify. 'I do not develop,' says Jakob von Gunten in *Jakob von Gunten*. 'I would prefer not to make any change,' says Bartleby. Their affinity reveals the similarity between silence and a certain decorative use of language."

Of the writers of the No, what we might call the scriveners' section is one of the strangest and the one that perhaps affects me the most. This is because, twenty-five years ago, I personally experienced the sensation of knowing what it is to be a copyist. And I suffered terribly. I was very young at the time and felt very proud to have published a book on the impossibility of love. I gave my father a copy without foreseeing the troublesome consequences that this would have for me. A few days later, my father, annoyed at what he perceived in my book to be a record of offences against his first wife, obliged me to write a dedication to her in the copy that I had given him, which he himself dictated. I resisted such an idea as best I could. Literature was precisely – the same was true for Kafka – the only means I had to try to become independent of my father. I fought like a madman not to have to copy what he wanted to dictate to me. But finally I gave in, it was dreadful to feel that I was a copyist under the orders of a dictator of dedications.

This incident had such a negative impact on me that I did not write anything for twenty-five years. Not long ago, a few days before hearing that Mr Bartleby was in a meeting, I read a book that helped reconcile me to my condition as a copyist. I believe that the laughter and enjoyment I derived from reading *Institute Pierre Menard* helped pave the way for my decision to be rid of the old trauma and go back to writing.

Institute Pierre Menard, a novel by Roberto Moretti, is set in a secondary school whose pupils are taught to say "no" to over a thousand proposals, ranging from the most ludicrous to the most attractive and difficult to turn down. The novel is written in a jocular vein and is a very clever parody of Robert Walser's *Jakob von Gunten*. In fact Walser himself and the scrivener Bartleby are among the school's pupils. Nothing much happens in the novel, except that, by the time they have completed their studies, all the pupils have been transformed into consummate and cheerful copyists.

I laughed a lot while reading this novel, I am still laughing. Right now, for example, I laugh while I write because it occurs to me that I am a scrivener. To fix the image better in my mind, I take one of Robert Walser's books and pick a sentence at random, which I copy down: "Over the now darkened landscape treks a solitary figure." I copy this sentence down and proceed to read it aloud with a Mexican accent, and chuckle softly to myself. And this reminds me of a story of copyists in Mexico: that of Juan Rulfo and Augusto Monterroso; for years they worked as clerks in a gloomy office where, as I understand, they behaved like pure Bartlebys, always afraid of their boss who was in the habit of shaking hands with his employees at the end of each day's work. Rulfo and Monterroso, copyists in Mexico City, would frequently hide behind a pillar because they thought that what their boss wanted was to say goodbye to them for good.

This fear of a handshake now brings to mind the story of the composition of *Pedro Páramo*, which its author, Juan Rulfo, explained in the following terms, revealing his human condition as a copyist: "In May 1954 I bought a school exercise book and jotted down the first chapter of a novel which for years had been taking shape inside my head [. . .]. I still do not know where the intuitions that gave rise to *Pedro Páramo* came from. It was as if someone dictated it to me. Suddenly, in the middle of the street, an idea would occur to me and I would note it down on scraps of green and blue paper."

After the success of the novel that he wrote as if he were a copyist, Rulfo wrote nothing else in thirty years. His case has often been compared to that of Rimbaud, who, having published his second book at the age of nineteen, abandoned everything and went off in search of adventure, until his death two decades later.

For a time, the panic he felt that his boss's handshake might mean the sack coexisted with the fear of people coming up to him to tell him that he had to publish again. When they asked him why he no longer wrote, Rulfo would say,

"Well, my Uncle Celerino died and it was he who told me the stories."

His Uncle Celerino was no fabrication. He existed in real life. He was a drunk who made a living confirming children. Rulfo frequently accompanied him and listened to the fabulous stories he related about his life, most of which were invented. The stories of *El llano en llamas* almost had the title *Los cuentos del tío Celerino* (Tales of Uncle Celerino). Rulfo stopped writing shortly before his uncle's death. The excuse of his Uncle Celerino is one of the most original I know among all those concocted by the writers of the No to justify their abandonment of literature.

"You ask why I do not write?" Juan Rulfo was heard to remark in Caracas in 1974. "It is because my Uncle Celerino died and it was he who told me the stories. He was always chatting to me. But he was full of lies. Everything he told me was pure lies and so, naturally, what I wrote was pure lies. Some of the things he chatted to me about had to do with the misery in which he had lived. But Uncle Celerino was not so poor. Given that he was a respectable man, in the opinion of his local archbishop, he was appointed to tour the different towns confirming children. These were dangerous lands and the priests were afraid of them. I frequently accompanied

Uncle Celerino. Each place we arrived in, he had to confirm a child and then he charged for the confirmation. I have yet to write all of this down, perhaps I'll eventually get round to doing it. It's interesting how we moved from town to town confirming children, bestowing God's blessing on them and so on, don't you think? Especially considering he was an atheist."

But Juan Rulfo did not only have the story of his Uncle Celerino to justify his not writing. Sometimes he would resort to smokers of pot.

"Now," he would comment, "even smokers of pot publish books. There've been a lot of very strange books recently, don't you think? I have preferred to keep silent."

Concerning Juan Rulfo's mythical silence, Monterroso, his good friend in the office of Mexican copyists, has written an ingenious fable, "The Wisest Fox". In it, there is a certain Fox, who produced two successful books and with good reason was prepared to stop there, and the years went by and he did not publish any more. The others started to gossip and to wonder out loud what had happened to the Fox and when they met him at a cocktail party they would go up to him and tell him that he had to publish again. "But I've already published two books," the Fox would say wearily. "And they're very good," they would answer, "which is why you should publish another." The Fox would not say so, but he thought that what people really wanted was for him to publish a bad book. But, because he was the Fox, he refused.

Transcribing Monterroso's fable has finally reconciled me to the good fortune of being a copyist. Farewell, trauma brought about by my father. There is nothing horrible about being a copyist. When one copies something, one belongs to the line of Bouvard and Pécuchet (Flaubert's characters) or of Simon Tanner (with his creator Walser in the shadows) or of Kafka's anonymous court officials.

To be a copyist is also to have the honour of belonging to the constellation of Bartleby. Filled with joy, I lowered my head a few moments ago and became lost in other thoughts. I was at home, but I fell half asleep and was transported to an office of copyists in Mexico City. Desks, tables, chairs, armchairs. In the background, a large window through which, rather than being seen, fell a fragment of the Comala landscape. And further back, the exit door with my boss extending his hand. Was it my boss in Mexico or my real boss? Brief confusion. I was sharpening pencils, and I realized that it would take me no time at all to hide behind a pillar. The pillar reminded me of the folding screen behind which Bartleby continued to hide after the Wall Street office in which he lived had already been dismantled.

I said to myself suddenly that, if someone were to discover me behind the pillar and want to find out what I was doing there, I would cheerfully tell them that I was the copyist who worked with Monterroso, who in turn worked for the Fox.

"Is Monterroso, like Rulfo, a writer of the No as well?"

I thought I could be asked this question at any time and so I was ready with the answer:

"No. Monterroso writes essays, cows, fables and flies. He doesn't write much, but he writes."

Having said this, I woke up. I was then overcome by a huge desire to record my dream in this book of footnotes. A copyist's happiness.

That is enough for today. I shall carry on with my foot-notes tomorrow. As Walser wrote in *Jakob von Gunten*, "I must stop writing for today. It excites me too much. The letters flicker and dance in front of my eyes."

2) If the excuse of Uncle Celerino was a justification of some substance, the same could be said of that used by the Spanish writer Felipe Alfau not to write again. This gentleman, who was born in Barcelona in 1902 and died a few months ago in a New York retirement home, found in what happened to him as a Latin learning English the ideal justification for his prolonged literary silence of fifty-one years.

Felipe Alfau emigrated to the States during the First World War. In 1928 he wrote his first novel, *Locos: A Comedy of Gestures*. The following year, he published a children's book, *Old Tales from Spain*. Then he fell into a silence akin to that of Rimbaud or Rulfo. Until, in 1948, he published *Chromos*, which was followed by an impressive and definitive literary silence.

Alfau, a kind of Catalan Salinger, sought refuge in a retire-ment home in Queens and, in the best style of elusive authors, informed journalists trying to interview him at the end of the eighties, "Mr Alfau is in Miami."

In *Chromos* – in terms reminiscent of those used by Hofmannsthal in his emblematic text of the No, the "Letter of Lord Chandos" (in which the latter gives up writing because he says he has completely lost the ability to think or speak coherently about anything) – Felipe Alfau explains his decision to stop writing in the following way: "The moment one learns English, complications set in. Try as one may, one cannot elude this conclusion, one must inevitably come back to it. This applies to all persons, including those born to the language and, at times, even more so to Latins, including Spaniards. It manifests itself in an awareness of implications and intricacies to which one had never given a thought; it afflicts one with that officiousness of philosophy which, having no business of its own, gets in everybody's way and, in the case of Latins, they lose that racial characteristic of taking things for granted and leaving them to their own devices without inquiring into causes, motives or ends, to meddle indiscreetly into reasons which are none of one's affair and to become not only self-conscious, but conscious of other things which never gave a damn for one's existence."

I am very impressed by the "Uncle Celerino" Felipe Alfau pulled out of his hat. It strikes me as most ingenious to say that one has given up writing as a result of the distress of having learnt English and become aware of intricacies to which one had never given a thought.

I have just mentioned this to Juan, who is possibly the only friend I have, although we see little of each other. Juan loves reading – it helps him to relax after his job at the airport, which has got him down at the moment – and he believes that since Musil no-one has written a single good novel. He had only heard of Felipe Alfau and had no idea that he had used the drama of having learnt English to justify his decision to stop writing. When I told him about it today over the phone, he burst out laughing. Then he began to say to himself over and over again, with evident enjoyment,

"You mean English overcomplicated things for him . . ."

Finally I hung up. I had the impression that I was wasting

my time with him and should go back to my book of footnotes. I did not bother feigning depression with Juan. I did feign a deep depression with Social Security and was granted sick-leave for three weeks (since I've holidays in August, I won't have to go to the office until September), which will allow me to devote all my energies to this diary, I can devote all my time to these cherished notes on Bartleby's syndrome.

I hung up, then, on the man who after Musil rates nobody, and returned to my affairs, to this diary. Suddenly it occurred to me that Samuel Beckett, like Alfau, ended up in a retirement home and that, like Alfau, he entered the home of his own volition.

I found something else the two of them had in common. It seemed to me very possible that English overcomplicated things for Beckett as well, and this would explain his famous decision to start using French, a language he considered better suited to his writing, because it was poorer and more simple.

3) "I grew used," writes Rimbaud, "to simple hallucination: I saw very clearly a mosque in place of a factory, a school of drummers formed by angels, carriages on the highways of the sky, a salon at the bottom of a lake."

At the age of nineteen, Rimbaud, with amazing precociousness, had already completed his works and fell into a literary silence that would last until the end of his days. Where did his hallucinations originate from? I believe they came to him simply from a very powerful imagination.

Less clear is where the hallucinations of Socrates came

from. Although it has always been known that he had a delirious and hallucinatory character, a conspiracy of silence has ensured that this was kept in the dark for centuries. The fact that one of the pillars of our civilisation should have been an unbridled eccentric was not an easy pill to swallow.

Until 1836 no-one dared to recall the real personality of Socrates; it was Louis Francisque Lélut in a beautiful essay, "Du démon de Socrate", who, basing his essay scrupulously on the testimony of Xenophon, dared to redress the image of the Greek sage. Sometimes one could almost be looking at a portrait of the Catalan poet Pere Gimferrer: "He wore the same coat in all seasons, he walked barefoot on the ice and on the earth warmed by the Greek sun, he danced and jumped frequently on his own, with no motive, as if on a whim [. . .], in short, owing to his conduct and manners, he gained the reputation of being such a misfit that Zeno the Epicurean nick-named him 'the Attic buffoon', what today we would term an 'eccentric'."

Plato offers a rather disturbing account of Socrates' delirious and hallucinatory character in the *Symposium*: "On the way Socrates fell into his own private thoughts and kept dropping behind. I stopped to wait for him, but he told me to go on ahead [. . .]. 'No,' I said to the others, 'leave him. He does this very often, he suddenly comes to a halt and stands there.' 'I perceived,' Socrates said suddenly, 'that divine sign which is familiar to me, the appearance of which always stops me in my tracks [. . .]. The god governing me has not allowed me to talk to you of it until now, and I was waiting for his permission.'"

"I grew used to simple hallucination" is something Socrates could have written as well, were it not for the fact that he never wrote a single line; his mental excursions of a hallucinatory nature may have had a lot to do with his rejection of writing. No-one can derive much pleasure from the task of making a written inventory of their own hallucinations. Rimbaud did it, but after two books he grew tired, perhaps because he sensed that he was going to lead a very bad life if he spent all his time recording his incessant visions one by one. Rimbaud may have been aware of that story by Asselineau, "The Musician's Hell", which tells of the terrible hallucination endured by a composer condemned to hear all his compositions performed both well and badly on all the pianos in the world simultaneously.

There is an evident relationship between Rimbaud's refusal to continue making an inventory of his visions and the perpetual literary silence of a hallucinating Socrates. However, we might, if we wish, see Rimbaud's emblematic decision to stop writing as simply repeating the historic gesture of a silent Socrates, who did not bother to write books like Rimbaud, but went straight to the point, and from the start declined to write down all his hallucinations as if heard on all the pianos in the world.

The following words of Victor Hugo could well be applied to this relationship between Rimbaud and his illustrious predecessor Socrates: "There are some mysterious men who can only be great. Why are they great? Even they do not know. Might He who has sent them know? They possess a terrible vision in their eyes that never abandons them. They have seen the ocean like Homer, the Caucasus like Aeschylus, Rome like Juvenal, the inferno like Dante, paradise like Milton, man like Shakespeare. Drunk with fantasy and intuition in their almost unconscious advance over the waters of the abyss, they have crossed the strange line of the ideal, which has penetrated them for ever . . . A pale shroud of light covers their countenance. Their soul emerges through their pores. What soul? God."

Who sends these men? I do not know. Everything changes except God. "In six months even death changes fashion," Paul Morand observed. But God never changes, I tell myself. It is well known that God keeps quiet, is a master of silence, hears all the pianos in the world, is a consummate writer of the No, and for that reason He is transcendent. I could not agree more with Marius Ambrosinus, who said, "In my opinion, God is an exceptional person."

4) In reality the illness, Bartleby's syndrome, has a long history. Today it is a disease endemic to contemporary letters, this negative impulse or attraction towards nothingness that means that certain literary authors apparently never manage to be one.

In fact the twentieth century opens with Hofmannsthal's paradigmatic text (the "Letter of Lord Chandos" dates from 1902), in which the Viennese author promises, in vain, never again to write a single line. Franz Kafka is forever alluding to the essential impossibility of literary matter, particularly in his *Diaries*.

André Gide created a character who spends an entire novel intending to write a book which he never writes (*Paludes*). Robert Musil exalted and almost mythologised the idea of an "unproductive author" in *The Man Without Qualities*. Monsieur Teste, Valéry's alter ego, has not only refused to write, he has even thrown his library out of the window.

Wittgenstein published only two books: the famous *Tractatus Logico-philosophicus* and an Austrian rural vocabulary. On more than one occasion he made reference to the difficulty he had in expressing his ideas. Like Kafka, he produced a compendium of unfinished texts, sketches and plans for books he never published.

But one need only cast a glance at the literature of the nineteenth century to realise that "impossible" books and paintings are an almost logical inheritance of Romantic aesthetics. Francesco, a character in Hoffmann's *The Devil's Elixir*, never manages to paint a Venus he considers to be without blemish. In *The Unknown Masterpiece*, Balzac tells us of a painter who can only give shape to part of the foot of his perfect woman. Flaubert never completed his project *Le Garçon*, even though it directed his entire work. And Mallarmé only managed to scribble financial calculations on hundreds of quartos, and that was the sum of his projected great *Livre*.

So the modern spectacle of all these people paralysed before the absolute dimensions required by all creation has a long history. But, paradoxically, those who shun the pen constitute literature as well. As Marcel Bénabou writes in *Why I Have Not Written Any of My Books*, "Above all, dear reader, do not believe that the books I have not written are pure nothingness. On the contrary (let it be clear once and for all), they are held in suspension in universal literature."

5) Sometimes one stops writing because one simply falls into a state of madness from which one never recovers. The

best example of this is Hölderlin, who had an involuntary successor in Robert Walser. The former spent the last thirty-eight years of his life enclosed in the attic of the carpenter Zimmer, in Tübingen, writing strange and incomprehensible verses which he signed with the names Scardanelli, Killalusimeno and Buonarotti. The latter spent the last twenty-eight years of his life shut up in the mental hospitals first of Waldau and then of Herisau, engaged in a frenetic activity of microscopic handwriting, fictitious and indecipherable gibberish scrawled on minute pieces of paper.

I think it might be said that, in a certain way, both Hölderlin and Walser *carried on writing*. "To write," Marguerite Duras remarked, "is also not to speak. It is to keep silent. It is to howl noiselessly." Of Hölderlin's noiseless howls, we have the record of, among others, J. G. Fischer, who gives the following account of his final visit to the poet in Tübingen: "I asked Hölderlin to write some lines on any one topic, and he asked me if I would have him write on Greece, on Spring or on the Spirit of Time. I replied the last of these three. And then, with what might be described as a youthful fire burning in his eyes, he settled himself at his desk, took a large sheet of paper, a new pen, and began to write, marking the rhythm on his desk with the fingers of his left hand and expressing a hum of satisfaction at the end of each line while nodding his head in a gesture of approval . . ."

Of Walser's noiseless howls, we have the copious testimony of Carl Seelig, the loyal friend who continued to visit the writer when he ended up in the mental hospitals of Waldau and Herisau. Out of all the "portraits of a moment" (the literary genre Witold Gombrowicz was so fond of), I choose the one where Seelig caught Walser at the exact moment of truth, that instant when a person, with a gesture – Hölderlin's nodding of the head, for example – or a phrase, reveals who they really are: "I shall never forget that morning in autumn when Walser and I were walking together from Teufen to Speichen, through a thick fog. I told him that day that perhaps his work would last as long as Gottfried Keller's. He stood rooted to the spot, viewed me with utter seriousness and asked me, if I valued his friendship, never to repeat such a compliment. He, Robert Walser, was a walking nobody and he wished to be forgotten."

Walser's entire work, including his ambiguous silence of twenty-eight years, is a commentary on the vanity of all initiative, the vanity of life itself. Perhaps that is why he only wanted to be a walking nobody. Someone has compared Walser to a long-distance runner who is on the verge of reaching the longed-for finishing-line and stops in surprise, looks round at masters and fellow disciples, and abandons the race, that is to say remains in what is familiar, in an aesthetics of bewilderment. Walser reminds me of Piquemal, a curious sprinter, a cyclist in the sixties who suffered from mood swings and would sometimes forget to finish a race.

Robert Walser loved vanity, the fire of summer, women's ankle boots, houses illumined by the sun, flags fluttering in the wind. But the vanity he loved had nothing to do with the drive for personal success, rather it was the sort that is a tender display of what is minimal, what is fleeting. Walser could not have been further from the heady heights, where power and prestige dominate: "Were a wave to lift me and carry me to the heights, where power and prestige are predominant, I would destroy the circumstances that have favoured me and hurl myself downwards, to the vile, insignificant darkness. Only in the lower regions am I able to breathe."

Walser wanted to be a walking nobody and what he most desired was to be forgotten. He realised that every writer must be forgotten almost as soon as he has stopped writing, because the page has been lost, has literally flown away, has entered a context of different situations and sentiments, answers questions put by other men, which its author could not even have imagined.

Vanity and fame are ridiculous. Seneca claimed that fame is horrible because it depends on the judgement of many. But this is not exactly what made Walser desire to be forgotten. More than horrible, worldly fame and vanity were, to him, completely absurd. This was because fame, for example, seems to assume that there is a proprietorial relationship between a name and a text that now has an existence, yet which that pallid name can surely no longer influence.

Walser wanted to be a walking nobody, and the vanity he loved was like that of Fernando Pessoa, who once, on throwing a chocolate silver-foil wrapper to the ground, said that, in doing so, he had thrown away life.

Someone else who laughed at worldly vanity, at the end of his days, was Valéry Larbaud. While Walser spent the last twenty-eight years of his life shut up in mental hospitals, Valéry Larbaud, owing to a stroke, spent the last twenty years of his eventful existence in a wheelchair.

Larbaud remained lucid and lost none of his memory, but his language became chaotic, lacking in syntactical organization, reduced to nouns or isolated infinitives, and he fell into a worrying silence which one day, out of the blue, to the surprise of some friends who had come to visit him, he broke by saying, "*Bonsoir les choses d'ici bas.*"

Good evening to the things here below? An untranslatable sentence. Hector Bianciotti, in a story dedicated to Larbaud, observes that in *bonsoir* there is twilight, the dying day, instead of night, and a subtle irony colours the sentence in the reference to *the things here below*, meaning of this world. To replace it with *goodbye* would alter the delicate nuance.

Larbaud repeated the sentence at various points during the day, permanently stifling his laughter, no doubt to show that he was not deluded, that he knew the sentence meant nothing at all, but that it was very effective as a commentary on the vanity of all initiative.

At the other extreme, we find Fanil, protagonist of "The Vain Man", a story by an Argentinian writer I greatly admire, J. Rodolfo Wilcock, a consummate author who in turn greatly admired Walser. I have just come across an interview hidden in the pages of one of his books, in which Wilcock makes this declaration of principles: "Among my preferred authors are Robert Walser and Ronald Firbank, and all the authors preferred by Walser and Firbank, and all the authors these authors preferred."

Fanil, the main character in the story, has transparent skin and muscles, so much so that it is possible to distinguish the various organs in his body, as if they were enclosed in a glass case. Fanil loves to exhibit himself and to exhibit his viscera, he receives friends dressed only in a pair of swimming trunks, he leans out of the window revealing a naked torso; he allows everyone the opportunity to admire the operations of his organs. His two lungs fill with air, his heart beats, his digestive tract contorts slowly, and he is unashamed. "This is always the case," writes Wilcock. "When someone has a peculiarity, instead of hiding it, they make a show of it, and sometimes go so far as to make it their raison d'être."

At the conclusion of the story, we are told that all this goes on until eventually someone says to the vain man, "Hey, what's that white patch under your nipple? It wasn't there before." And so we see the outcome of parading oneself distastefully.

6) Some people decide not to write because of a conviction that they are nobody. Pepín Bello, for example. Marguerite Duras said, "The story of my life does not exist. There is no centre. There is no path or line. There are wide open spaces where someone was supposed to be, but it's not true, there was nobody." "I am nobody," says Pepín Bello when he is interviewed and reference is made to his proven role as galvaniser or architect, prophet or brains behind the generation of '27, and above all behind the group which he, García Lorca, Buñuel and Dalí formed in the Residencia de Estudiantes. In *La edad de oro*, Vicente Molina Foix tells how, when he reminded Bello of his decisive influence on the best talents of his generation, he merely answered, with a modesty that sounded neither hollow nor proud, "I am nobody."

However much one talks to Pepín Bello – today a nonagenarian and a surprising writer of the No despite his artistic genius – however much one reminds him that all the memoirs and books dealing with the generation of 27 re-echo with his name, however much one tells him that in all these books he is spoken of in terms of the highest esteem for his ideas, far-sightedness and wit, however much one asserts that he was the brains behind the most brilliant literary generation to come out of Spain in the twentieth century, however much one insists on all this, he always replies that he is nobody, and then, laughing in an infinitely serious way, he makes the following clarification: "I have written a great deal, but kept none of it. I have mislaid letters and texts dating from the time of the Residencia de Estudiantes, because I didn't think they were worth anything. I have written memoirs and torn them up. The genre of memoirs is important, but I am not."

In Spain, Pepín Bello is the perfect example of someone who declined to write, the inspired archetype of the Spanish artist without works. Bello is listed in all the dictionaries of art, he is credited with an exceptional activity, and yet he has no works, he has passed through the history of art with no ambition to make it to the top: "I have never written in order to be published. I did it for my friends, to have a laugh, for a bit of fun."

Once, when I was visiting Madrid some five years ago, I stopped by the Residencia de Estudiantes, where a conference had been organized in honour of Buñuel. Pepín Bello attended. I spied on him for a good while and even went up to him to hear what kind of things he was saying. I heard him, with playful amusement, say this:

"I'm the Pepín Bello of the manuals and dictionaries."

I shall never cease to be amazed by the destiny of this recalcitrant writer of the No, whose unassuming nature is always being highlighted, as if he knew that this was the real way to distinguish oneself.

7) Bobi Bazlen commented, "I believe it is no longer possible to write books. That is why I no longer write them. Virtually all books are no more than footnotes, inflated until they become volumes. That is why I write only footnotes."

His *Note senza testo* (Notes Without a Text), collected in notebooks, were published in 1970 by the Adelphi publishing house, five years after his death.

Bobi Bazlen was a Jew from Trieste who had read every book in every language and who, while possessing a very demanding literary conscience (or perhaps precisely because of this), instead of writing preferred to intervene directly in people's lives. The fact that he never wrote a book forms part of his work. Bazlen, a kind of black sun of the crisis in the West, is an extremely curious case; his very existence seems to signal the true end of literature, of the absence of output, the death of the author: a writer without books and therefore books without a writer.

But why didn't Bazlen write?

This is the question on which Daniele Del Giudice's novel *Wimbledon Stadium* centres. From Trieste to London, this question steers the investigation of the narrator (the novel is written in the first person), a young man who queries Bazlen's decision, fifteen years after his death, and travels to Trieste and London in search of friends from his youth, who are now elderly. He questions the mythical writer of the No's old friends in search of the reasons why – when he could have done so magnificently – he never wrote a book. Bazlen, who has since sunk into obscurity, was very famous and revered in Italian publishing circles. This man, who was supposed to have read every book, advised Einaudi and backed Adelphi from its foundation in 1962, he was a friend to Svevo, Saba, Montale and Proust, and introduced Freud, Musil and Kafka, among others, into Italy.

All his friends spent their lives believing that Bazlen would end up writing a book and that it would be a masterpiece. But Bobi Bazlen left only his footnotes, *Notes Without a Text*, and an unfinished novel, *Master Mariner*.

Del Giudice has pointed out that, when he started writing *Wimbledon Stadium*, he hoped to keep Bazlen's idea in the text that "it is no longer possible to carry on writing," but at the same time he sought to give this negative statement a twist. He knew that this way he would make the narrative more tense. What eventually happened to Del Giudice at the end of his novel is easy to predict: he saw that the whole novel was simply just the account of a decision, the decision to write. There are even moments in the book when Del Giudice treats the mythical writer of the No with extreme cruelty, quoting what an old friend of Bazlen has said: "He was evil. He spent his whole time meddling in other people's lives and affairs. He was nothing but a failure who lived his life through others."

Elsewhere in the novel, the young narrator has this to say: "Writing is not important, but that's all there is to do." Thus the narrator proclaims a moral directly opposed to Bazlen's. "Almost timidly," Patrizia Lombardo has written, "Del Giudice's novel contradicts those who fault literary or architectural production, all those who revere Bazlen for his silence. Between the triviality of pure artistic creativity and the terror of negativity, perhaps there is room for something different: the moral of form, the pleasure of a well-crafted object."

It seems to me that Del Giudice regards writing as a high-risk activity and in this sense, following in the footsteps of Pasolini and Calvino, understands the written text to be founded on nothingness; a text, if it wishes to be valid, must open up new paths and try to say what has not yet been said.

I think I am in agreement with Del Giudice. A well-crafted description, though it be obscene, has a moral ingredient: the will to tell the truth. The use of language simply for effect paradoxically constitutes an immoral act. In *Wimbledon Stadium* Del Giudice's search is ethical precisely because he struggles to create new forms. The writer who attempts to push back the frontiers of what is human may fail. However, the author of conventional literary products never fails, runs no risks, all he need do is apply the same old formula, that of the comfortable academic, that of concealment.

Just as in the "Letter of Lord Chandos" (in which we are told that the infinite cosmic whole of which we are part cannot be described in words, which means that writing is a small and insignificant mistake, so small it makes us almost mute), Del Giudice's novel illustrates the impossibility of writing, but also points us to the potential for new ways of looking at new objects, so that it is better to write than not to do so.

Are there any other reasons for thinking it is better to write? Yes. One of them is very simple: because it is still possible to write in the classical style with a heightened sense of the risk and of beauty. This is the great lesson to be drawn from Del Giudice's book, since in it, on page after page, there is a profound interest in the antiquity of the new. Because the past always re-emerges with a twist. The Internet, for example, is new, but the *net* has always existed. The net fishermen used for catching fish serves now not to enclose prey, but to open up the world to us. Everything remains, but changes; the everlasting is repeated mortally in the new, which is gone in a flash.

8) Are there any other reasons for thinking it is better to write? I have just read *The Truce* by Primo Levi, in which the author describes the people he was with in a concentration camp, people we would know nothing about were it not for this book. Levi tells how they all wanted to return to their homes, how they wanted to continue living, not just out of the instinct for survival, but because they wished to recount what they had seen. They wanted their experience to prevent all this happening again, but there was more: they sought to explain their tragedy so that it might not sink into obscurity.

We, all of us, wish to rescue, via memory, each fragment of life that suddenly comes back to us, however unworthy, however painful it may be. And the only way to do this is to set it down in writing.

Literature, as much as we delight in denying it, allows us to recall from oblivion all that which the contemporary eye, more immoral every day, endeavours to pass over with absolute indifference.

*   *   *

9) If Plato thought that life was a forgetting of the idea, Clément Cadou spent his whole life forgetting that he once had the idea of wanting to be a writer.

His strange attitude – to forget about writing, he would spend his whole life considering himself a piece of furniture – has similarities to the no less strange biography of Félicien Marboeuf, a writer of the No I discovered in *Artistes sans oeuvres* (Artists Without Works), an ingenious book by Jean-Yves Jouannais on the subject of creators who chose not to create.

Cadou was fifteen years old when his parents invited Witold Gombrowicz to their house for dinner. It was only a few months (this was at the end of April 1963) since the Polish writer had embarked from Buenos Aires for the last time and, having paid a lightning visit to Barcelona, had come to Paris, where, among many other things, he had accepted the invitation to dine with the Cadous, old friends of his from the fifties in Buenos Aires.

The young Cadou had aspirations to be a writer. In fact he had already dedicated months to preparing for it. His parents were delighted and, unlike many others, had placed every facility at his disposal so that he could be a writer. They were thrilled that their son might one day be transformed into a brilliant star of the French literary firmament. The boy was not lacking in talent, he was a voracious reader of all kinds of books and he worked conscientiously to become an admired writer in the shortest time possible.

At his tender age, the young Cadou was reasonably familiar with Gombrowicz's work, which had impressed him a great deal and which led him sometimes to recite whole paragraphs from the Polish writer's novels in front of his parents.

And so the parents' satisfaction at inviting Gombrowicz to dinner was twofold. They were excited at the prospect of their young son having direct contact, in the comfort of their own home, with the genius of the great Polish author.

But something very unexpected occurred. The young Cadou was so awestruck on seeing Gombrowicz within the four walls of his parents' home that he hardly said a word all evening and ended up – something similar had befallen the young Marboeuf when he saw Flaubert in his parents' home – feeling literally like a piece of furniture in the drawing room where they had dinner.

As a result of this domestic metamorphosis, the young Cadou saw how his aspirations to become a writer were permanently rescinded.

But Cadou's case differs from that of Marboeuf in the frenetic artistic activity which, from the age of seventeen, he undertook to fill the gap left in him by his irreversible decision not to write. Unlike Marboeuf, Cadou did not merely see himself as a piece of furniture all his brief life (he died young); but at least he painted. And of course he painted furniture. It was his way of slowly forgetting that he had once wanted to write.

All his paintings centred exclusively on a piece of furniture and they all bore the same enigmatic and repetitive title: *Self-Portrait*.

"The thing is, I feel like a piece of furniture, and pieces of furniture, to the best of my knowledge, don't write," Cadou would say in his defence when reminded that as a boy he had wanted to be a writer.

There is an interesting study of Cadou's case by Georges Perec (*A Portrait of the Author Seen as a Piece of Furniture, Always,*

Paris, 1973), in which sarcastic emphasis is placed on what happened in 1972, when poor Cadou died after a long and painful illness. His relatives unwittingly buried him as if he were a piece of furniture, they got rid of him like some surplus furniture, and buried him in a niche near the Marché aux Puces in Paris, that market where so many old pieces of furniture are to be found.

Knowing that he was going to die, the young Cadou wrote a short epitaph for his tomb, which he asked his family to accept as his "complete works". An ironic request. The epitaph reads as follows: "I tried in vain to be other pieces of furniture, but even that was denied me. So I have been a single piece of furniture my whole life, which is, after all, no mean achievement when one considers that the rest is silence."

10) Not going to the office makes me live even more isolated than I already was. But this is no drama, quite the opposite. I now have all the time in the world, and this allows me – as Borges would say – to tire out shelves, to enter and leave the books in my library, always searching for new cases of Bartlebys that will allow me to add to the list of writers of the No which I have been compiling over so many years of literary silence.

This morning, while leafing through a dictionary of famous Spanish writers, I happened to come across a curious case of rejection of literature, that of the distinguished Gregorio Martínez Sierra.

This writer, whom I studied in school and who always

struck me as extremely dull, was born in 1881 and died in 1947, founded magazines and publishing houses, wrote terrible poems and awful novels, and was already on the verge of suicide (his failure could not have been more publicised) when he suddenly became famous as a writer of feminist plays – *The Mistress of the House* and *The Cradle Song* among others, not to mention *The Romantic Young Lady* – which took him to the pinnacle of glory.

Recent research suggests that all his theatrical works were written by his wife, María de la O Lejárraga, otherwise known as María Martínez Sierra.

11) It is no drama to live so isolated, but sometimes I do feel the need to communicate with someone. But, in the absence of friends (except for Juan) and other acquaintances, there is no-one I can turn to, nor would I particularly want to. All the same, in order to write this book of footnotes, I am aware that I could do with the collaboration of others who might extend the information I possess about Bartlebys, about writers of the No. Perhaps it is not enough for me to have a list of Bartlebys and to tire out shelves. This is what has led me this morning to take it upon myself to send a letter to Paris to Robert Derain, whom I've never met before, but who is the author of *Éclipses littéraires*, a magnificent anthology of short stories belonging to authors who have all written a single book in their lives and then renounced literature. All of the authors in this book of eclipses are inventions, just as the stories attributed to these Bartlebys were in fact written by Derain himself.

I have sent Derain a short letter, asking him if he would be so kind as to contribute to this book of footnotes. I have explained that this book will signify my return to writing after twenty-five years of literary eclipse. I have enclosed a list of those Bartlebys I have already tracked down and asked him to send me news of any writers of the No I may be missing.

I wonder what will happen.

12) Not writing anything because one is waiting for inspiration is a trick that always works, it was used by Stendhal himself, who says in his autobiography, "Had I mentioned to someone around 1795 that I planned to write, anyone with any sense would have told me to write for two hours every day, with or without inspiration. Their advice would have enabled me to benefit from the ten years of my life I totally wasted waiting for *inspiration*."

There are many tricks for saying *no*. If anyone ever gets round to writing a history of the art of refusal in general (not just of the refusal to write), they should bear in mind a delicious book recently published by Giovanni Albertocchi, *Disagi e malesseri di un mitente*, in which a study is carried out with supreme wit into the sophistries articulated by Manzoni in his collected letters as a way of saying *no*.

Thinking about Stendhal's sophistry has reminded me of one used by that strange and disturbing poet Pedro Garfias, during his exile in Mexico, not to write. Luis Buñuel, in his memoirs, describes him as a man who could spend ages not writing even a single line, because he was searching for an adjective. Whenever Buñuel saw him, he would ask him,

"Have you found that adjective yet?"

"No, I'm still searching," Pedro Garfias would reply before moving off pensively.

Another, no less ingenious, device is that contrived by Jules Renard, who in his *Diary* notes this down: "You'll achieve nothing. However much you do, you'll achieve nothing. You understand the best poets, the most profound prose-writers, but though they say to understand is to equal, you'll be about as comparable to them as the lowest dwarf can be compared to giants [. . .] You'll achieve nothing. Weep, shout, clasp your head in both your hands, hope, lose hope, apply yourself again, push the stone. You'll achieve nothing."

There are lots of tricks, but it is also true to say that there have been several writers who refused to contrive a justification for their decision not to write; these writers vanished physically, leaving no clues, and so they never needed to explain why they did not wish to write any more. When I say "physically", I do not mean that they took their own lives, simply that they vanished, they decamped without trace. Of these writers, notable examples are Crane and Cravan. They sound like an artistic duo, but they weren't, they never even met; however, they do have one point in common: the two of them vanished in Mexican waters under mysterious circumstances.

Just as it was said of Marcel Duchamp that his finest work was his use of time, so it might be said of Crane and Cravan that their finest work was their disappearance without trace in Mexican waters.

Arthur Cravan claimed that he was Oscar Wilde's nephew and, apart from editing five issues of a magazine in Paris called *Maintenant*, he did nothing else. Although he barely lifted a finger, the five issues of *Maintenant* were more than enough for him to take a place with full honours in the history of literature.

In one of these issues, he wrote that Apollinaire was a Jew. The latter rose to the bait and sent a protest to the magazine denying it. Then Cravan wrote a letter of apology, probably already aware that his next move would be to travel to Mexico and there to disappear without trace.

When one is aware that one is going to disappear, one is not very diplomatic with the people one most detests.

"Though I am not afraid of Apollinaire's sabre," he wrote in the final issue of *Maintenant*, "given that I have very little *amour propre*, I am prepared to set the record straight in every way and to declare that, contrary to what I may have suggested in my article, Apollinaire is not a Jew, but a Roman Catholic. In the hope of avoiding possible future misunderstandings, I should like to add that the aforementioned gentleman has a large belly, his outward appearance is closer to that of a rhinoceros than to that of a giraffe [. . .]. I should also like to rectify a sentence that may give rise to misinterpretations. When I say, in reference to Marie Laurencin, that somebody should lift up her skirts and stick a large *** up a certain part, what I mean is that somebody should lift up Marie Laurencin's skirts and stick a large astronomy up her music hall."

He wrote this and left Paris. He travelled to Mexico, where he boarded a canoe one afternoon and said that he would return in a few hours. That was the last anyone ever saw of him, his body was never found.

As for Hart Crane, it should be said first of all that he was born in Ohio, the son of a rich industrialist, and that as a child he was much affected by his parents' separation, which produced in him a deep emotional wound that led him to be always skirting the peaks of madness.

He believed that the only possible way out of his drama was through poetry, and for a time he steeped himself in poetry, it was even claimed that he had read every poem in the world. This may explain the huge demands he made on himself when it came to undertaking his own poetical work. He was greatly disturbed by the cultural pessimism he saw in T. S. Eliot's *The Waste Land*, which he thought was taking lyric verse to a dead end precisely in the space, that of poetry, in which he had glimpsed the only possible means of escape from his dramatic experience as the child of separated parents.

He wrote *The Bridge*, an epic poem for which he received endless praise, but, given the demands he made on himself, he was not satisfied, being of the opinion that he could scale much higher peaks in poetry. It was then that he decided to travel to Mexico with the idea of writing an epic poem like *The Bridge* but which had a greater depth of meaning, since this time the chosen theme was Moctezuma. However, the figure of this emperor (who very quickly struck him as excessive, colossal, totally beyond his reach) ended up causing him serious mental disorders which prevented him from writing the poem, and convinced him – as Franz Kafka had been convinced years before, without knowing it – that the only thing one could write about was indeed very depressing; he said to himself that one could only write about the essential impossibility of writing.

One afternoon he embarked in Veracruz for New Orleans. Embarkation meant for him giving up poetry. He never arrived in New Orleans, he vanished somewhere in the Gulf of Mexico. The last person to see him was John Martin, a businessman from Nebraska, who was talking to him on the ship's deck about trivial matters when Crane mentioned Moctezuma and his face adopted an alarming air of humiliation. In an attempt to conceal his sudden sombre appearance, Crane quickly changed the subject and asked if it was true that there were two New Orleans.

"To the best of my knowledge," replied Martin, "there's the modern city and the one that isn't."

"I shall visit the modern city and from there walk to the past," said Crane.

"Do you like the past, Mr Crane?"

He did not answer the question. Looking even more sombre than a few seconds before, he moved off slowly. Martin thought that, if he bumped into him again on deck, he would reiterate the question whether he liked the past. But that was the last he saw of him, that was the last anyone saw of Crane, he vanished in the depths of the Gulf. When the others disembarked in New Orleans, he was no longer there, not even for the art of refusal.

13) Since I began these notes without a text, I have been hearing as background noise something that Jaime Gil de Biedma wrote about not writing. Without a doubt, his words further complicate the labyrinthine theme of the No: "Perhaps I should say a little more about this, about not writing. A lot of people ask me about it, and I ask myself. And asking myself why I do not write inevitably leads to another, much more unsettling question: why did I ever write? After

all, the normal thing is to read. I have two preferred answers. The first, that my poetry was – without my knowledge – an attempt to create an identity for myself; having created and assumed this identity, I was no longer concerned to throw myself into every poem I set about writing, which is what fascinated me. The other, that it was all a mistake: I believed that I wanted to be a poet, but deep down I wanted to be a poem. And to a degree, an unfortunate degree, I have achieved this; like any reasonably well-crafted poem, I now lack inner freedom, I am all need and internal submission to that tormented tyrant, that insomniac, omniscient and ubiquitous Big Brother: Me. Half Caliban, half Narcissus, I fear him most when I hear him interrogate me, next to an open balcony: 'What's a boy of 1950 like you doing in an indifferent year like this?' All the rest is silence."

14) I would give anything to own Alonso Quijano's impossible library or Captain Nemo's. All the books in these two libraries are held in suspension in universal literature, as are the books from Alexandria's library, those 40,000 scrolls which were lost in the fire started by Julius Caesar. The story goes that, in Alexandria, the wise Ptolemy devised a letter "to all the Sovereignties and Governors on Earth", in which he thought to ask them "not to hesitate to send him every kind of written work [. . .] by poets and historians, doctors and inventors, astrologers, mathematicians and geniuses". Apart from that, we know that Ptolemy ordered a copy to be made of all the books found in ships putting in at Alexandria, the originals to be retained and their owners to

be handed the copies. This collection he later named "the ships' collection".

All of this has disappeared, fire appears to be a library's final destiny. But though so many books have disappeared, they are not pure nothingness; on the contrary, they are held in suspension in universal literature, as are all Alonso Quijano's books of chivalry or the mysterious philosophical treatises in Captain Nemo's underwater library – Don Quixote's and Nemo's books are "the ship's collection" of our most intimate imagination – as are all the books that Blaise Cendrars wanted to bring together in a volume he planned over a long period and very nearly wrote: *Manuel de la bibliographie des livres jamais publiés ni même écrits.*

Another phantom library – except that it exists and can be visited at any time – is the Brautigan Library, which is in Burlington, USA. This library is named after Richard Brautigan, an American underground writer, author of such works as *The Abortion, Trout Fishing in America* and *Willard and His Bowling Trophies.*

The Brautigan Library accepts exclusively manuscripts that, having been rejected by the publishers who were sent them, were never published. This library holds only aborted books. Anyone with such a manuscript, wishing to submit it to the Brautigan Library or Library of the No, need only pop it in the post to the town of Burlington in Vermont, USA. I have it on good authority – though there they are only interested in bad authority – that no manuscript is ever rejected; on the contrary, there they are looked after and exhibited with the greatest pleasure and respect.

⋆   ⋆   ⋆

15) In the mid-seventies I worked in Paris, and from those days I can clearly remember María Lima Mendes and the strange Bartleby's syndrome that had her gripped, paralysed, terrified.

I fell in love with María as I have never fallen in love with anybody, but she was not interested, she treated me simply as the work colleague that I was. María Lima Mendes had a Cuban father and a Portuguese mother, a blend she was especially proud of.

"Somewhere between the Cuban song and the Portuguese *fado*," she used to say, smiling with a hint of sadness.

When I started working at Radio France Internationale and met her, María had already been living in Paris for three years. Before that she had divided her time between Havana and Coimbra. María was delightful, she had an extraordinary mestizo beauty, she wanted to be a writer.

"A 'literata'," she used to specify, her Cuban wit tinged with the shade of the *fado*.

It is not because I was in love with her that I say it: María Lima Mendes is one of the most intelligent people I have ever met. And, without a doubt, one of the most gifted for the art of writing. When it came to inventing stories, she had a prodigious imagination. Pure Cuban wit and Portuguese sadness. What can have happened for her not to become the "literata" she wanted to be?

The afternoon I met her in the corridors of Radio France, she was already seriously *touchée* by Bartleby's syndrome, by the negative impulse that had subtly been driving her to a total paralysis in the face of writing.

"The Evil One," she used to say, "it is the Evil One."

The source of this evil, according to María, could be traced to the irruption of *chosisme*, an unfamiliar word to me in those days.

"*Chosisme*, María?"

"*Oui*," she would reply, nodding and then relating how she had arrived in Paris at the start of the seventies and had moved into the Latin Quarter with the idea that this district would very quickly transform her into a "literata", since she was well aware that successive generations of Latin American writers had lived in the district and happily encountered there the ideal conditions to be writers. María would quote Severo Sarduy, who said that, since the beginning of the century, these writers had not found exile in France or in Paris, but in the Latin Quarter and two or three of its cafés.

María Lima Mendes spent hours in the Flore or in the Deux Magots. I often managed to sit with her; she treated me with great sensitivity as a friend, but she did not love me, she did not love me at all, though she was fond of me because she pitied my hump. I would often while away the time pleasantly, sitting next to her. And more than once I heard her remark that, when she arrived in Paris, moving into that district had signified for her, to start with, joining a clan, becoming part of a coat of arms, something like embracing a secret order and accepting a burden of continuity, being marked by the heraldry of alcohol, absence and silence; these were the principal emblems of the literary quarter and its two or three cafés.

"Why do you say absence and silence, María?"

Absence and silence, she explained to me one day, because she was often affected by her nostalgia for Cuba, the murmur of the Caribbean, the sickly-sweet fragrance of the guava, the purple shade of the jacaranda, the reddish stain, shading the siesta, of a royal poinciana and, above all, by the voice of Celia Cruz, the familiar voices of childhood and partying.

Despite the absence and silence, in the beginning Paris was one long party for her. Becoming part of a coat of arms and embracing the secret order took a dramatic turn at the point when the Evil One appeared in María's life, preventing her from becoming a "literata".

In its first stage, the Evil One bore the name *chosisme*.

"Chosisme, María?"

Chosisme. Bossa nova had not been to blame, but *chosisme*. When she arrived in the district at the start of the seventies, it was fashionable in novels to dispense with the argument. The in thing was *chosisme*: the morbid description of objects – a table, a chair, a penknife, an inkpot . . .

All of this, in the long run, would end up harming her a great deal. But when she arrived in the district she cannot even have suspected this. As soon as she moved into the rue Bonaparte, she got down to work and began to frequent the district's two or three cafés and immediately began to write an ambitious novel at the tables of those cafés. The first thing she did, therefore, was accept the burden of continuity. "You cannot be unworthy of those who come before," she said, referring to the other Latin American writers who in the distance gave her, at tables outside those cafés, consistency, texture. "Now it's my turn," she would say to herself on her first, enthusiastic visits to those tables, where she started writing her first novel, which had a French title, *Le cafard*, though she was going to write it in Spanish of course.

She started the novel very well, following a preconceived plan. In it, a woman with an unmistakable air of melancholy was sitting in one of a row of folding chairs, next to some other, elderly passengers, silent, impassive, gazing at the sea. Unlike the sky, the sea displayed its usual dark grey tone. But it was calm, the waves made a quiet, soothing sound as they broke softly on the sand.

They were in sight of land.

"I have the car," said the man in the chair next to her.

"This is the Atlantic, isn't it?" she asked.

"That's right. Why, what did you think it was?"

"I thought it might be the Bristol Channel."

"No, no. Look." The man took out a map. "Here's the Bristol Channel, and here we are. This is the Atlantic."

"It's very grey," she commented, and asked a waiter for a very cold mineral water.

So far so good for María, but, from the moment the woman asked for a mineral water, the novel ran dramatically aground and María suddenly decided to practise *chosisme*, to kowtow to fashion. She devoted no fewer than thirty pages to a precise description of the label on the bottle of mineral water.

By the time she finished this exhaustive description of the label and returned to the waves breaking softly on the sand, the novel was so blocked as to be destroyed, she could not go on with it, which disheartened her so much that she buried herself in her new job at Radio France. If she had only buried herself in that . . ., but she also decided to undertake a thorough study of the novels that formed the *nouveau roman*, which is where *chosisme* attained its apotheosis, in particular in the work of Robbe-Grillet, and it was Robbe-Grillet María read and analysed the most.

One day she decided to pick up *Le cafard*. "The boat seemed to be making no progress . . ." Thus began her new attempt

41

to be a novelist, but she started it aware that she was carrying a dead weight: Robbe-Grillet's obsession with doing away with time and lingering unnecessarily on trivia.

Although something told her that it would be better to opt for a plot and recount a story as so many had done before her, something also firmly held her back and told her that she would be seen as an uncouth, reactionary novelist. The idea of such an accusation horrified her, and finally she decided to continue with *Le cafard* in the most unadulterated Robbe-Grilletian style: "The pier, which seemed further away on account of the perspective, gave off parallels on either side of the main line and these, with a precision further pronounced by the morning light, marked out a series of elongated, alternately horizontal and vertical planes: the solid parapet . . ."

It did not take her long, writing like this, to become totally paralysed again. Once more she buried herself in her work, and it was at that time she met me, a writer who was similarly paralysed, though for different reasons to hers.

María Lima Mendes' *coup de grâce* came from the magazine *Tel Quel*.

In the texts of this magazine, she saw her salvation, the chance to go back to writing and, what is more, to do it in the only way possible, the only correct way, "trying," she once said to me, "to bring about the ruthless dismantling of fiction."

But very soon she ran into a serious problem involved in writing this kind of text. However much she armed herself with patience when it came to analysing the construction of texts by Sollers, Barthes, Kristeva, Pleynet & Co., she could not quite understand what it was that these texts were proposing. And, to make matters worse, when she did from time to time understand what these texts were saying, she felt even more paralysed when it came to starting to write because what they were saying, after all, was that there was nothing else to write and there was nowhere even to begin saying that it was impossible to write.

"Where to begin?" María asked me one day, sitting at a literary table outside the Flore.

Both terrified and confused, I did not know what to say to encourage her.

"All that's left is to finish," she answered herself aloud, "to give up once and for all any idea of creativity, of authoring texts."

The final blow came from a text by Barthes – "Where to begin?" no less.

This text unbalanced her, caused her irreparable, decisive damage.

One day she handed it to me and I have kept it.

"There is," Barthes has to say among other pleasantries, "an operational malaise, a simple difficulty, which corresponds to all rudiments: *where to begin?* In its practical guise with its gestural charm, we might say that this difficulty is the same which founded modern linguistics: suffocated initially by the heteroclite nature of human language, Saussure, to put an end to that oppression, which is in short that of the *impossible beginning*, decided to take a thread, a pertinence (that of meaning), and wind it. Thus a system of language was constructed."

Unable to lay hands on this thread, María, who was unable to understand, among other things, what exactly it meant to be "suffocated initially by the heteroclite nature of human language" and was finding it more and more difficult to know *where to begin*, ended up falling definitively silent as a writer and desperately reading Tel Quel and not understanding it. A real tragedy, because a woman as intelligent as she was did not deserve this.

I stopped seeing María Lima Mendes in 1977, when I came back to Barcelona. It was only a few years ago that I had news of her again. My heart skipped a beat, proving to me that I was still fairly in love with her. A work colleague from that time in Paris had traced her to Montevideo, where María was working for France Presse. He gave me her telephone number. And I rang her and almost the first thing I asked her was whether she had conquered the Evil One and finally been able to devote herself to writing.

"No, darling," she told me. "That bit about the *impossible beginning* really struck home with me. There's nothing we can do."

I asked her if she had been aware of the publication in 1984 of a book, *Ghosts in the Mirror*, which attributed the origins of the *nouveau roman* to an imposture. I explained to her that this demythologisation had been written by Robbe-Grillet and seconded by Roland Barthes. And I told her that the devotees of the *nouveau roman* had preferred to look the other way, given that the author of the exposé was none other than Robbe-Grillet. In the book he describes the ease with which he and Barthes discredited the notions of author, narrative and reality, and refers to all that manoeuvring as "the terrorist activities of those years".

"No," María said with the same old cheerfulness and a hint of sadness. "I hadn't realised. Maybe I should join an association of victims of terrorism. All the same, it doesn't change anything. Besides, I'm glad they were only con men, it says a lot for them, and I just love fraud in art. Why delude ourselves, Marcelo? I couldn't write now even if I wanted to."

Possibly because I was planning this book of footnotes about writers of the No, the last time I spoke to her, about a year ago, I reverted to my theme – "now that the technical and ideological watchwords of objectivism and other folderol have disappeared," I said somewhat sarcastically – and asked her again whether she had not thought of writing *Le cafard* or any other novel which might justify the passion for a plot.

"No, darling," she said. "I still think what I thought before, I still ask myself where to begin, I'm still paralysed."

"But, María . . ."

"It's not María any more. I've changed my name to Violet Desvarié. I shan't write a novel, but at least I'll sound like a novelist."

16) Recently it is as if the writers of the No had decided to come out and meet me. I was watching a bit of television this evening, minding my own business, when I came across a documentary on Barcelona Television about a poet called Ferrer Lerín, a man of about fifty-five who in his early years lived in Barcelona, where he was friends with the then up-and-coming poets Pere Gimferrer and Félix de Azúa. He wrote some very daring, rebellious poems during that period – both Azúa and Gimferrer said in the documentary – but at the end of the sixties he dropped everything and went to live in Jaca, Huesca, a very provincial town with the added draw-back that it is a military garrison. Had he not left Barcelona

so soon, he would most probably have been included in Castellet's anthology *Nueve novísimos*. But he moved to Jaca, where he has devoted the last thirty years to the systematic study of vultures. He is, therefore, a vulturologist. He reminds me of the Austrian author Franz Blei, who spent his time cataloguing his literary contemporaries in a bestiary. Ferrer Lerín is an expert on birds, he studies vultures, perhaps today's poets as well, most of whom are vultures. Ferrer Lerín studies birds which feed on dead flesh – or poetry. His destiny seems to me at least as fascinating as Rimbaud's.

17) Today is 17 July, it is two o'clock in the afternoon and I am listening to Chet Baker, my favourite musician. A while ago, when I was shaving, I looked in the mirror and did not recognise myself. The radical loneliness of these last few days is turning me into someone else. Nevertheless, I am enjoying the anomaly, the deviation, the monstrosity of myself as an isolated individual. I derive a certain pleasure from being unfriendly, from swindling life, from adopting the posture of literature's radical non-hero (which is to say from playing at being like the cast of these footnotes), from observing life and seeing that the poor thing lacks a life of its own.

I looked in the mirror and did not recognise myself. Then I fell to thinking about what Baudelaire used to say, that the real hero is he who keeps himself amused. I looked in the mirror again and detected a certain resemblance to Watt, Samuel Beckett's reclusive character. Like Watt, I could be described in the following way: a bus stops opposite three repugnant old men, who watch it seated on a public bench. The bus moves off. "Look," says one of them, "someone's left a bundle of rags." "No," says the second, "that is a fallen rubbish bin." "Not at all," says the third, "it is a pile of old newspapers that's been put there." At that moment the heap of rubbish advances towards them and asks them extremely impolitely to move up. This is Watt.

I don't know if I should have written "heap of rubbish". I don't know. I am full of doubts. Perhaps I should terminate my excessive isolation. Talk to Juan at least, call him at home and ask him to tell me again how after Musil there is nobody. I am full of doubts. The only thing I am suddenly now sure of is that I must change my name and call myself AlmostWatt. Oh, I don't know how important it is that I say this or something else. Saying is inventing. Be it false or certain. We invent nothing, we think we are inventing when in fact all we are doing is stammering out the lesson, the remains of some homework learnt and forgotten, life without tears, just as we weep over it. And to hell with it.

I am only a written voice, virtually without a private or public life, I am a voice that throws out words which fragment by fragment compose the long history of Bartleby's shadow over contemporary literature. I am AlmostWatt, I am mere discursive flow. I have never aroused passions, and I am not likely to arouse them now that I am only a voice. I am AlmostWatt. I let them say, my words, which are not mine, I, that word, that word they say, but they say it in vain. I am AlmostWatt and in my life there have only ever been three things: the impossibility of writing, the possibility of it, and loneliness, physical of course, which now takes me forward. Out of the blue I hear someone saying to me,

"AlmostWatt, can you hear me?"

"Who goes there?"

"Why don't you forget about your mess and talk about the case of Joseph Joubert, for example?"

I look and there is nobody, and I tell the ghost that I am at its service, I tell it this and then I laugh, and I end up keeping myself amused, like real heroes.

18) Joseph Joubert was born in Montignac in 1754 and died seventy years later. He never wrote a book. He only prepared himself to write one, single-mindedly searching for the right conditions. Then he forgot this purpose as well.

In his search for the right conditions to write a book, Joubert discovered a delightful place where he could digress and end up not writing a book at all. He almost put down roots during his search. And the point is, as Blanchot says, what he was searching for, the source of all writing, that space where he could write, that light which ought to be circumscribed in space, demanded of him and confirmed in him dispositions which made him unsuitable for any ordinary literary work or distracted him from the same.

In this respect Joubert was one of the first totally modern writers, preferring the centre to the sphere, sacrificing results in order to discover their conditions, and not writing in order to add one book to another, but to seize control of the point from which all books seemed to him to originate, which, once attained, would exempt him from writing them.

However, it is still curious that Joubert should not have written a book, since he was, from very early on, only attracted by and interested in what was being written. From a very young age he had been drawn to the world of books that were going to be written. In his youth he was very close to Diderot, afterwards to Restif de la Bretonne, both of whom produced abundant works. In his later years almost all his friends were famous writers with whom he lived immersed in the world of letters and who, knowing his immense literary talent, encouraged him to break his silence.

The story goes that Chateaubriand, who exerted great influence over Joubert, came up to him one day and remarked, "Ask that prolific writer lurking inside you to stop being so damn prejudiced, will you?"

By that time Joubert had already digressed in his search for the source of all books and was already clear that, were he to locate that source, he would be exempted from writing a book.

"I can't yet," he replied to Chateaubriand, "I still haven't found the source that is the object of my search. But if I do find it, I shall have even more reason not to write that book you would have me write."

While he searched and amused himself in his digressions, he kept a secret diary of a purely personal nature, which he had no intention of ever publishing. But his friends behaved badly towards him and, on his death, took the liberty in dubious taste of publishing this diary.

It has been said that Joubert did not write his long-awaited book because he thought the diary was enough. Such a claim seems to me preposterous. I do not believe that Joubert was taken in, seeing in his diary a substitute for literary abundance. The pages of his diary served simply to express the numerous ups and downs he went through in his heroic quest for the source of all writing.

There are priceless moments in his diary as when, at the age of forty-five, he writes, "But what is my art exactly? What goal does it aspire to? What do I hope to achieve by practising it? Is it to write and to know that others are reading me? Sole ambition of so many! Is that what I want? This is what I must investigate stealthily and at length until I uncover the answer."

In his stealthy and prolonged search, he always acted with admirable lucidity and never lost sight of the fact that, even as an author without a book and a writer without texts, he still moved in the field of art: "Here I am, detached from civil things, in the pure region of art."

More than once he saw himself as taken up with a task more fundamental to art, and of greater essential interest, than a work: "One must resemble art without resembling a single work."

What was this essential task? Joubert would not have liked someone saying they knew what this essential task consisted of. In reality Joubert understood that he was looking for what he did not know, hence the difficulty of his search and the joy of his discoveries as a digressive thinker. Joubert wrote in his diary. "But how to look in the right place when one does not even know what one is looking for? This happens whenever one composes and creates. Fortunately, by digressing, one does not simply make a discovery, one has happy encounters."

Joubert knew the happiness of the art of digression, of which he was possibly the founder.

When Joubert says he is uncertain about the essence of his strange task as a digressive, he reminds me of what happened to György Lukács once when, surrounded by his followers, the Hungarian philosopher was being showered with praise regarding his work. Overwhelmed, Lukács made the remark, "Yes, yes, but now I see that I have not understood the crux of the matter." "And what is that?" they asked him in surprise. To which he responded, "The trouble is I don't know."

Joubert – who wondered how to look in the right place when one does not even know what one is looking for – reflects in his diary on the difficulties he had finding a refuge or adequate space for his ideas: "My ideas! I can't seem to manage to build a house where they can live."

Such an adequate space he may have imagined as a cathedral which would fill the entire firmament. An impossible book. Joubert foreshadows Mallarmé's ideals: "It would be tempting," writes Blanchot, "and at the same time glorious for Joubert to see in him an untranscribed first edition of Mallarmé's *Un coup de dés*, of which Valéry said, 'It finally raised a page to the potential of the starry sky.'"

Joubert's dreams and the work produced a century later share a common ambition: the desire (in both Joubert and Mallarmé) to replace ordinary reading, where it is necessary to go from one part to another, with the spectacle of a simultaneous word, in which everything would be said at once without confusion, in a glow that is – to quote Joubert – "total, peaceable, intimate and uniform at last".

So it was that Joseph Joubert spent his life searching for a book he never wrote, though, when all is considered, he wrote it without realising, thinking of writing it.

19) I woke up very early and, while I was preparing breakfast, I was thinking about all the people who do not write

and it suddenly occurred to me that in fact more than ninety-nine per cent of humanity prefer, in the most unadulterated style of Bartleby, not to, prefer not to write.

It must have been this impressive figure that set my nerves on edge. I began to imitate the gestures Kafka would sometimes use: clapping, rubbing my hands together, shrugging my shoulders, lying on the ground, jumping, preparing to throw or catch something . . .

Thinking of Kafka reminded me of the Hunger Artist in one of his stories. This artist refused to ingest any food because for him it was obligatory to fast, he could not avoid it. I thought for a moment of when the inspector asks him why he cannot avoid it and the Hunger Artist, raising his head and whispering in the inspector's ear so that none of his words is lost, replies that he was always forced to fast because he could never find any food he liked.

And then I remembered another artist of the No, who also appears in a story by Kafka. I thought of the Trapeze Artist, who refused to touch the ground with his feet and spent day and night on the trapeze, never coming down, remaining suspended twenty-four hours a day, in the same way that Bartleby never left the office, not even on a Sunday.

After thinking about these clear examples of artists of the No, I observed that I was still somewhat jittery and agitated. I said to myself that it would do me good to get out a bit, not to limit myself to greeting the porter, to discussing the weather with the newspaper man or to responding with a laconic no in the supermarket when the checkout girl asks me whether I have a member card.

It occurred to me that, overcoming my shyness as far as possible, I could conduct a small survey among ordinary people into why they do not write, in an attempt to find out which is the "Uncle Celerino" each of them has.

Around noon I took up position in the newspaper/book-shop on the corner. A lady was reading the back cover of a book by Rosa Montero. I walked up to her and, after a short preamble with which I sought to gain her confidence, I asked her almost point-blank,

"So why don't you write?"

Women sometimes display the most devastating logic. She looked at me in surprise, smiled and said,

"You amuse me. Tell me, why do you think I should write?"

The bookseller listened in to the conversation and, when the woman had left, said to me,

"Trying it on so soon?"

His conspiratorial look annoyed me. I decided to turn my attention to him and I asked him why he did not write.

"I prefer to sell books," he replied.

"Less effort, I suppose," I said with rising indignation.

"To tell you the truth, I should like to write in Chinese. I love adding up and making money."

This disconcerted me.

"What do you mean?" I asked him.

"Oh, nothing. It's just that if I'd been born in China, I shouldn't have minded writing. The Chinese are very clever, they write letters from top to bottom as if they were then going to add up what they've written."

This incensed me. And what's more, his wife, standing next to him, laughed at her husband's joke. I bought one newspaper less from them than usual and asked her why she did not write.

She sank into thought, and for a moment I nourished the

hope that her response might be more illustrative than those I had obtained previously. In the end she said,

"Because I don't know."

"What don't you know?"

"How to write."

In view of its success, I left the survey for another day. On returning home, I read in a newspaper some surprising declarations by Bernardo Atxaga, in which the Basque writer says he has lost the appetite to write: "After twenty-five years on the road, as singers say, I'm finding it increasingly difficult to work up an appetite to write."

Atxaga is quite clearly showing the first symptoms of Bartleby's syndrome. "Recently," he remarks, "a friend suggested to me that to be a writer nowadays requires more physical strength than imagination." In his opinion, there are too many conferences, conventions, interviews and book launches. He questions to what extent the writer needs to appear in society and in the media. "It used to be fairly innocuous," he says, "but now it's become essential. I sense an atmosphere of change around me. I see one type of author disappearing, like Leopoldo María Panero, who could once be placed in a kind of Salon des Indépendants. The way literature is publicised has changed as well. As have the literary prizes, which are a joke and a deceit."

In view of all this, Atxaga proposes to write one more book and to retire. An outcome the author does not consider at all dramatic. "There's no reason it should be sad, it's simply a reaction to change." He ends by saying that he is going to call himself Joseba Irazu again, which was his name when he decided to write under the pseudonym of Bernardo Atxaga.

I was delighted by the rebellious gesture contained in the announcement of his retirement. I remembered Albert Camus: "What is a rebel? A man who says *no*."

Then I pondered over the change of name and recalled Canetti, who said that fear invents names as a distraction. Claudio Magris, commenting on this statement, says that this would explain why, when we travel, we read and note down names in the stations we leave behind, with the simple purpose of finding some relief on our journey, some satisfaction in this order and rhythm of nothingness.

Enderby, Anthony Burgess' character, travels noting down the names of stations, but ends up in a mental hospital, where they cure him by changing his name, because, as his psychiatrist points out, "Enderby was the name of a prolonged adolescence."

Similarly I invent names as a distraction. Since calling myself AlmostWatt, I feel happier. Though I've still got the jitters.

20) I have pretended that Derain wrote to me. Given that the author of *Éclipses littéraires* does not deign to answer my letter, I have decided to write one to myself, signing it from Derain.

My dear friend: I suspect that what you're really after is my blessing on your appropriation of my idea of writing about people who give up writing. Am I not on the right track? Well, you needn't worry. If what you want is for me not to protest the evident plagiarism of my idea, rest assured that, when you publish your book, I shall behave as if you had skilfully bought my silence. You see, I've taken a liking to you, so much so that I'm even going to give you a Bartleby you're missing.

Include Marcel Duchamp in your book.

Just like you, Marcel Duchamp had few ideas. Once, in Paris, the artist Naum Gabo asked him directly why he had stopped painting. "*Mais que voulez-vous?*" Duchamp replied, spreading wide his arms, "*je n'ai plus d'idées*" (What do you expect? I've no more ideas).

In time he would provide other, more sophisticated explanations, but this one was probably closest to the truth. After *The Large Glass*, Duchamp had run out of ideas, so instead of repeating himself he simply stopped creating.

Duchamp's life was his finest work of art. He abandoned painting very early on and embarked on a daring adventure in which art was conceived, first and foremost, as a *cosa mentale*, in the spirit of Leonardo da Vinci. He wanted always to place art at the service of the mind and it was precisely this desire – driven by his particular use of language, by chance, optics, films and, above all, by his famous "readymades" – which stealthily undermined 500 years of Western art and transformed it completely.

Duchamp abandoned painting for over fifty years because he preferred to play chess. Isn't that wonderful?

I imagine you are perfectly aware who Duchamp was, but let me remind you of his activities as a writer; let me relate how Duchamp helped Katherine Dreier form her own personal museum of modern art called the Société Anonyme, Inc., advising her what art works to collect. When plans were made to donate the collection to Yale University in the forties, Duchamp wrote thirty-three one-page biographical and critical notices on artists from Archipenko to Jacques Villon.

Roger Shattuck has written in the *New York Review of Books* that had Marcel Duchamp decided, not uncharacteristically, to include a notice on himself as one of Dreier's artists, he would probably have produced an astute blend of truth and fable, like the others he wrote. Roger Shattuck suggests that he might have written something along these lines:

"A tournament chess player and intermittent artist, Marcel Duchamp was born in France in 1887 and died a United States citizen in 1968. He was at home in both countries and divided his time between them. At the New York Armory Show of 1913, his *Nude Descending a Staircase* delighted and offended the press, provoked a scandal that made him famous *in absentia* at the age of twenty-six, and drew him to the United States in 1915. After four exciting years in New York City, he departed and devoted most of his time to chess until about 1954. A number of young artists and curators in several countries then rediscovered Duchamp and his work. He had returned to New York in 1942 and during his last decade there, between 1958 and 1968, he once again became famous and influential."

Include Marcel Duchamp in your book about Bartleby's shadow. Duchamp knew that shadow personally, he made it with his own hands. In a book of interviews, Pierre Cabanne asks him at one point if he undertook any artistic activity during those twenty summers he spent in Cadaqués. Duchamp answers that he did, since every year he had to repair an awning that sheltered him on his terrace. I admire him greatly and, what's more, he's a man who brings luck – include him in your treatise on the No. What I most admire about him is that he was a first-rate trickster.

Sincerely, Derain.

21) We have learnt to respect tricksters. In his note for an unwritten preface for *The Flowers of Evil*, Baudelaire advised the artist not to reveal his innermost secrets – and thus revealed his own: "Does one show to a now giddy, now indifferent public the working of one's devices? Does one explain all those revisions and improvised variations, right down to the way one's sincerest impulses are mixed in with tricks and with the charlatanism indispensable to the work's amalgamation."

In such a passage, charlatanism comes very close to becoming a synonym of "imagination". The best novel that has been written about charlatanism and that portrays a con man – *The Confidence-Man*, 1857 – is by Herman Melville, the great inspiration, ever since he created Bartleby, behind the intricate labyrinth of the No.

In *The Confidence-Man*, Melville conveys a latent admiration for the human being who can metamorphose himself into multiple identities. The stranger on Melville's riverboat performs a wonderfully Duchampian prank on himself (Duchamp was a prankster and loved pure verbal fantasy, among other reasons because he did not really believe very much in words, he was full of adoration for Jarry, the founder of pataphysics, and for the great Raymond Roussel), a prank on the other passengers and on the reader by posting "a placard nigh the captain's office, offering a reward for the capture of a mysterious impostor, supposed to have recently arrived from the East; quite an original genius in his vocation, as would appear, though wherein his originality consisted was not clearly given".

No-one ever catches up with Melville's strange impostor, just as nobody ever caught up with Duchamp, the man who did not trust in words: "As soon as we start putting our thoughts into words and sentences everything gets distorted, language is just no damn good – I use it because I have to, but I don't put any trust in it. We never understand each other." No-one ever caught up with the trickster Duchamp, whose cool achievement lay, beyond his works of art and non-art, in the wager that he could dupe the art world into honouring him on the basis of forged credentials, which he won. This is no easy task. Duchamp decided to lay a wager with himself about the artistic and intellectual culture to which he belonged. This great artist of the No wagered that he could win the game sitting down, hardly lifting a finger. And he won. He laughed at all those inferior con men we've become so accustomed to recently, at all those small-time con men who seek their reward not in laughter and the game of the No, but in money, sex, power or conventional fame.

This laughter accompanied Duchamp as he climbed up on stage at the end of his life to take his bow before an audience who admired his extraordinary ability to fool the art world with the minimum of effort. He climbed up on stage and the author of *Nude Descending a Staircase* did not even have to look down at the steps. From long and careful calculation, the great con man knew exactly where they were. He had planned it all, like the great master of the No he was.

22) Let us turn our attention to two writers who live in the same country, but who hardly know each other. The first has Bartleby's syndrome and has refused to carry on publishing; he has not published in twenty-three years. The second, without there being a reasonable explanation, endures the fact that the other does not publish as if it were a constant nightmare.

This is the case of Miguel Torga and his strange relationship with the Bartlebyan syndrome affecting the poet Edmundo de Bettencourt, a writer born in Funchal on the island of Madeira in 1899; he was a Law student in Coimbra, the city in which he became highly renowned as a singer of *fados*, something that undoubtedly tarnished the reputation he carved out for himself when, on leaving behind a period of Bohemian idleness, he began to publish exceptional books of poetry. For a time he did not weary of publishing his innovative and tragic verses. His best book appeared in 1940, *Poemas surdos*, containing pieces of high poetry such as *Nocturno fundo*, *Noite vazia* and *Sepultura aérea*. It was the pitiful reception of this book that plunged Bettencourt into a long period of silence that lasted twenty-three years.

In 1960 the Lisbon magazine *Pirâmide* tried to rescue the poet from his silence and took the liberty of devoting almost the entire magazine to him with a commentary on his poems of yesteryear. Bettencourt kept quiet. In true Bartlebyan style, he was unwilling to write even a few lines for this issue of the magazine devoted to him. *Pirâmide* justified the poet's decision to remain silent as follows: "Let it be clear that Bettencourt's silence is neither a capitulation nor an expression of dissent from current Portuguese poetry, but a personal form of revolt which he warmly defends."

1960 was a bad time for Portuguese poetry, which was dominated – as was happening in Spain on account of the dictatorship – by an aesthetics of socialist realism. In 1963 things had not changed, but Bettencourt agreed for his poems from the thirties, his poems of yesteryear and the maltreated verses, to be published again in a single volume. Despite the combative prologue by a young Herberto Helder, or perhaps because of it, the poems were once more abused. Oblivious to all this, but emerging from a long tunnel, Miguel Torga writes a charming letter to Bettencourt from Oporto, in which he reveals the following: "There are no new poems, but the old ones are there, and this alone has filled me with happiness. Your not publishing, dear sir, had become for me a real nightmare."

Despite the letter, Bettencourt would die ten years later, having published no more. "Edmundo de Bettencourt," someone wrote in the newspaper *República*, "passed away yesterday in a whisper. For the last thirty-three years, the poet had chosen not to sing at all, as if he had placed a mute over his life."

Did his death, the definitive silence of the poet from Madeira, signal the end of Torga's nightmare?

★   ★   ★

23) In between yawns I was flicking through a literary supplement in Catalan when I suddenly came across an article by Jordi Llovet, seemingly written in the hope of being included in this book of footnotes.

In his article, a literary review, Jordi Llovet more or less confesses that he gave up being a literary creator on account of his complete lack of imagination. It is not usual for a critic in a review to go about confessing that he suffers from Bartleby's syndrome. No, it is not usual at all. And as if that were not enough, the article contains a reference to a book by the English essayist William Hazlitt (1778–1830), who judging by the title of one of his texts – "A Farewell to Essay-Writing" – must have been, like Jordi Llovet, a fanatic of the No.

"William Hazlitt," writes Llovet, "literally saved my life. A few years back I had to travel from New York to Washington with the well-known and almost always efficient railway company Amtrak, and prior to the departure of the train I sat in the station waiting room, reading a collection of essays by this good man [. . .]. I was so caught up in the chapter "A Farewell to Essay-Writing" that I missed my train. That train was derailed somewhere near Baltimore with many casualties. A tragedy. And so why was I so captivated by this text? Perhaps even then I secretly intended to act on my vague desire never to write literary criticism again and to devote myself either to writing literature – Utopian daydream in a being so lacking in imagination as I am – or, without more ado, to pursuing a career in teaching, reading and, above all, in bibliophily, which is what I have ended up doing in the totally irrelevant and very simple life I lead . . ."

I had no idea that such pearls were to be found in this literary supplement. It's not at all usual for a critic, in the middle of reviewing a book, to talk to us about himself and to tell us point-blank that he renounced literary creation on account of his limited imagination – one needs imagination to say that, by the way – and not just that, but to succeed in moving us with his tale of the irrelevant and very simple life he leads.

Really it has to be recognised that having the imagination to say he has no imagination – Jordi Llovet's private "Uncle Celerino" – is a sensible excuse not to write, it's very well thought out, quite a discovery. Not like others who seek out exotic "Uncle Celerinos" to justify their militancy in the delicate army of writers of the No.

24) Last Sunday in July, rainy. It reminds me of a rainy Sunday Kafka recorded in his *Diaries*: a Sunday when the writer, because of Goethe, feels invaded by a complete inability to write and spends the day staring at his fingers, in the grip of Bartleby's syndrome.

"So the peaceful Sunday goes by," writes Kafka, "so the rainy Sunday goes by. I am sitting in the bedroom and I have silence to spare, but instead of settling down to write, an activity that the day before yesterday, for example, I would have thrown myself into with everything I've got, for a while now I've been staring at my fingers. I think this week I've been totally under the influence of Goethe, I think I have exhausted the energy of this influence and that is why I've become useless."

Kafka writes this on a rainy Sunday in January 1912. Two pages further on, in an entry dated 4 February, we discover that he is still trapped by the Evil One, by Bartleby's syndrome. We receive full confirmation that Kafka's "Uncle Celerino", at least for a good number of days, was Goethe: "the uninterrupted enthusiasm with which I read things about Goethe (conversations with Goethe, years as a student, hours with Goethe, a visit by Goethe to Frankfurt) and which prevents me from doing any writing".

There is the proof, if anyone was in doubt, that Kafka suffered from Bartleby's syndrome.

Kafka and Bartleby are two fairly unsociable characters I have tended to associate for some time. Of course I am not the only one to have felt tempted to do this. In fact Gilles Deleuze, in *Bartleby or the Formula*, says that Melville's copyist is the very image of the Bachelor, spelt with a capital letter, who appears in Kafka's *Diaries*, the Bachelor for whom "Happiness is the understanding that the ground on which he has stopped cannot be bigger than the area covered by his feet", the Bachelor who knows how to resign himself to a space that for him is growing smaller; the Bachelor the exact measurements of whose coffin, when he dies, will be just what he needs.

Along the same lines, I am reminded of other descriptions of the Bachelor, by Kafka, which also seem to be building up the very image of Bartleby: "He walks about with his jacket securely fastened, with his hands in his pockets, which are too high, his elbows sticking out, his hat pulled over his eyes, a false smile, innate by now, which must be to protect his mouth, just as his glasses protect his eyes; his trousers are tighter than is aesthetically pleasing on a pair of spindly legs. But everyone knows what is happening to him and can enumerate all his sufferings."

From the cross between Kafka's Bachelor and Melville's copyist I can picture a hybrid whom I am going to call Scapolo (*bachelor* in Italian) and who is related to that curious animal – "half kitten, half lamb" – inherited by Kafka.

Do we know what is happening to Scapolo? Well, I would say that a blast of coldness blows from within him, where he shows the sadder side of his double countenance. This blast of coldness derives from an innate and incurable disorder of the soul. It lays him at the mercy of an extreme negative impulse that causes him always to pronounce a resounding NO that is as if he were drawing it in capital letters in the quiet air of any rainy Sunday afternoon. This blast of coldness means that the more Scapolo withdraws from the living (for whom he works at times as a slave, at others as a clerk), the less space others consider necessary for him.

Scapolo seems good-natured like the Swiss (like the lack-adaisical Walser) and he resembles the classic man without qualities (like Musil), but we have already seen that Walser only appeared to be good-natured and that the appearances of the man without qualities are not to be trusted. In reality Scapolo is frightening, because he walks straight through a terrible zone, a zone of shadows which is also where the most radical of denials has its home and where the blast of coldness, in short, is a blast of destruction.

Scapolo is a stranger to us, half Kafka and half Bartleby, living on the edge of the horizon of a very distant world: a bachelor who says now that he would prefer not to, now, in a voice trembling like that of Heinrich von Kleist before his lover's grave, something as terrible and at the same time as simple as this:

"I'm not from here any more."

This is Scapolo's formula, quite an alternative to Bartleby's. I say this to myself while listening to the rain this Sunday blustering against the glass.

"I'm not from here any more," Scapolo whispers in my ear.

I smile at him with a certain fondness, and recall Rimbaud's "I am really from beyond the grave." I look at Scapolo and invent my own formula, and I also whisper in his ear, "I'm alone, bachelor." And then I can't help seeing myself as rather comical. Because it is comical to realise that one is alone while addressing another person.

25) From one rainy Sunday to another. I move to a Sunday in the year 1804, when Thomas De Quincey, who was then nineteen years old, took opium for the first time. Much later on, he would record that day in the following terms: "It was a Sunday afternoon, wet and cheerless: and a duller spectacle this earth of ours has not to show than a rainy Sunday in London."

In De Quincey Bartleby's syndrome manifested itself in the shape of opium. From the ages of nineteen to thirty-six, because of the drug, De Quincey was unable to write and would spend hours on end lying down, hallucinating. Before falling into the fantasies brought on by his strain of the Bartlebyan disease, he had declared his wish to be a writer, but nobody actually believed that he would do it, he had been given up as a lost cause, because opium surprisingly lifts the spirits of whoever ingests it, but befuddles the mind, albeit with bewitching ideas and pleasures. Obviously, if one is befuddled and bewitched, one cannot write.

But sometimes literature will shun drugs. And that is precisely what happened one fine day to De Quincey, who was able suddenly to rid himself of his strain of the disease. His way of overcoming it was original at the time, what he did was write directly about it. From where previously there was only opium smoke arose the celebrated treatise *Confessions of an English Opium Eater*, a seminal text in the history of drug-related literature.

I light a cigarette and, for a few moments, I pay tribute to opium smoke. I am reminded of Cyril Connolly's sense of humour when he summarised the biography of the man who overcame his disease by writing about it, but was unable to avoid the disease, which rebelled in the long run and killed him: "De Quincey: decadent English essayist who, at the age of seventy-five, was carried off by half a century of opium eating."

The smoke blinds my eyes. I know I should stop, that I've reached the end of this footnote. But I can hardly see, I can't go on writing, the smoke has dangerously turned into my own strain of the disease.

That's it. I've put the cigarette out. Now I can finish, and I shall do so with a quotation by Juan Benet: "Whoever needs to smoke in order to write must either imitate Bogart and have smoke curling around their eye (which leads to a rugged style), or else accept that the ashtray is going to consume most of the cigarette."

★   ★   ★

26) "Art is a stupidity," said Jacques Vaché, and then he killed himself, choosing the quick way to become an artist of silence. There won't be much room in this book for suicide Bartlebys, I'm not too interested in them, since I think that taking one's own life lacks the nuances, the subtle inventions of other artists – the game, in short, which is always more imaginative than a shot in the head – when called on to justify their silence.

I include Vaché in this book of footnotes, for him I make an exception, because I love his remark that art is a stupidity, and because it was he who revealed to me something that Susan Sontag discusses in her book *Styles of Radical Will*: "The choice of permanent silence doesn't negate [the artist's] work. On the contrary, it imparts retroactively an added power and authority to what was broken off – disavowal of the work becoming a new source of its validity, a certificate of unchallengeable seriousness. That seriousness consists in not regarding art [. . .] as something whose seriousness lasts for ever, an 'end', a permanent vehicle for spiritual ambition. The truly serious attitude is one that regards art as a 'means' to something that can perhaps be achieved only by abandoning art."

So I make an exception for the suicide Vaché, paradigm of the artist without works; he is listed in all the encyclopedias, though he wrote only a few letters to André Breton and nothing else.

And I'd like to make another exception for a genius of Mexican literature, the suicide Carlos Díaz Dufoo Jr. For this strange writer art is also a false path, an idiocy. In the epitaph from his bizarre *Epigrams* – published in Paris in 1927 and supposedly composed in this city, though later research shows that Carlos Díaz Dufoo Jr never left Mexico – he affirmed that his actions were dark and his words insignificant and he asked to be imitated. This out-and-out Bartleby is one of my greatest literary weaknesses and, despite committing suicide, he had to take his place in this book of footnotes. "He was a complete stranger among us," Christopher Domínguez Michael, the Mexican critic, has said of him. One has to be very strange indeed to appear strange to the Mexicans, who – at least so it seems to me – are so strange themselves.

I shall finish with one of his epigrams, my favourite epigram by Dufoo Jr: "In his tragic desperation he brutally tore the hairs from his wig."

27) I am going to make a third exception for suicides, and I'm going to make it for Chamfort. In a literary magazine, an article by Javier Cercas has set me on the track of a fierce supporter of the No: Monsieur Chamfort, who said that almost all men are slaves because they do not dare to articulate the word *no*.

As a man of letters, Chamfort was lucky from the start, he tasted success without making the slightest effort. The same was true of success in life. Women loved him, and his early works, mediocre though they were, ushered him into the salons, even arousing the royal fervour (Louis XVI and Marie Antoinette would cry uncontrollably at the end of performances of his works). It was not long before he entered the French Academy, and he enjoyed extraordinary social prestige at an early stage. However, Chamfort felt profound contempt for the world that surrounded him and he very quickly opposed his own personal advantages, with the natural consequences. He was a moralist, though not of the kind we have to put up with nowadays; Chamfort was not a hypocrite, he did not say that the world was horrendous only to save himself, he despised himself whenever he looked in the mirror: "Man is a stupid animal, judging by me."

His moralism was not fake, he did not use his moralism to gain the prestige of an upright man. "Our hero," Camus wrote about Chamfort, "will go even further, because the renunciation of his own advantages means nothing and the destruction of his body is unimportant (the way he committed suicide was savage), compared to the disintegration of his own spirit. This is, ultimately, what determines Chamfort's greatness and the strange beauty of the novel he did not write, but the necessary elements of which he left us so that we could imagine it."

He did not write that novel – he left *Maxims and Thoughts, Characters and Anecdotes*, but never novels – and his ideals, his radical No to the society of his time, drove him to a kind of desperate sainthood. "His extreme, cruel attitude," says Camus, "led him to that final denial which is silence."

In one of his *Maxims* we read the following: "M., whom they wanted to discuss various public and private matters, coldly replied, 'Every day I add to the list of things I don't talk about; the greatest philosopher would be the one with the longest list.'"

This will lead Chamfort to negate works of art and the pure force of language they contain, which he tried to communicate over such a long period. The denial of art led him to even more extreme denials, including that "final denial" referred to by Camus, who, commenting on why Chamfort did not write a novel and fell into an extended silence, has this to say: "Art is the opposite of silence, constituting one of the signs of that complicity which joins us to men in our common struggle. For someone who has lost that complicity and has sided *completely with rejection*, neither language nor art conserve their expression. This is, no doubt, the reason why that novel of a denial was never written: precisely because it was the novel of a denial. The point is that this art contains the very principles that ought to lead it to negate itself."

As we can see, Camus – a *yes*-artist if there ever was one in his firm belief that art is the opposite of silence – would have been somewhat paralysed had he known the work, for example, of Beckett and other consummate, recent disciples of Bartleby.

Chamfort took his *no* so far that, the day he thought that the French Revolution, which initially he had been enthusiastic about, had condemned him, he shot himself, breaking his nose and disgorging his right eye in the process. Still not dead, he returned to the attack, slitting his throat with a knife and cutting into his flesh. Bathed in blood, he stuck the knife into his chest and, after slashing his wrists and the backs of his knees, he collapsed in a vast pool of blood.

But, as has already been said, this was nothing compared to the disintegration of his spirit.

"Why don't you publish?" he had asked himself a few months earlier in a short text, "Products of the Perfected Civilisation".

From among his numerous answers, I have selected the following:

Because it seems to me that the public have the ultimate in bad taste and a desire for denigration.

Because we are encouraged to work for the same absurd reasons as when we look out of the window and hope to see monkeys and bear-tamers in the streets.

Because I am afraid to die without having lived.

Because the more my literary status declines, the happier I feel.

Because I do not want to imitate lettered people, who are like donkeys kicking and fighting in front of an empty manger.

Because the public are only interested in successes they do not appreciate.

28) I once spent a whole summer with the idea that I had been a horse. At night the idea became obsessive, it homed in on me. It was terrible. No sooner did I put my man's body to bed than my horse's memory came alive.

Of course I didn't tell anyone. Mind you, I didn't have anyone to tell, I've hardly ever had anyone. Juan was abroad that summer, otherwise I might have told him. I remember that I spent the summer on the trail of three women, none of whom paid me the slightest attention, they couldn't even spare me a minute to tell them something as intimate and terrifying as the story of my past, sometimes they wouldn't even look at me, I think my hump made them suspect that I had been a horse.

Juan called me today and I ended up telling him the story of that summer when I had a horse's memories.

"Nothing you say surprises me," he remarked.

This comment displeased me, and I regretted picking up the phone when Juan started leaving his message on the answering machine. As I've been receiving messages from him for days now – and from other people, whom I don't reply to either; I only pick up, sounding tremulous and depressed, when they phone from the office to enquire about my mental health – I thought it would be better to answer and tell Juan to leave me in peace, to stop pitying my hump and my loneliness as he has done all these years, and to respect these days of mine spent in the most radical isolation ever, because I need them to write my notes without a text. But I ended up telling him about my summer with a horse's memories.

He remarked that nothing I said surprised him, and went on to say that the story of that strange summer reminded him of the beginning of a story by Felisberto Hernández.

"What story?" I asked him, a little hurt that my original summer of yesteryear could not be exclusively mine.

"'The Woman Like Me'," he answered. "And now that I think about it, Felisberto Hernández bears some relation to what's been keeping you so busy. He never gave up writing, he's not a writer of the No, but his stories are. He didn't finish a single one, he liked to refuse to write an ending. His short story collection is called *Incomplete Narratives*. He left them all hanging in the air. The most marvellous of all his stories is 'No-One Turned the Lights On'."

"I thought you weren't interested in anyone after Musil," I said to him.

"Musil and Felisberto," he replied conclusively, very sure of himself. "Can you hear me properly? Musil and Felisberto. No-one turns the lights on after them."

Having got rid of Juan – which I did when he started telling me to make sure they didn't find out in the office that I was feigning depression and end up sacking me – I started rereading Felisberto's short stories. Certainly he was a writer of genius, he did his best to disappoint the expectations usually met in fiction. Bergson defined humour as a fruitless wait. This definition, which may be applied to literature as well, is fulfilled with rare thoroughness in the narrative of Felisberto Hernández, writer and also pianist in fashionable salons and seedy casinos, author of a fictional phantom space, writer of stories he did not finish (as if to indicate there's something missing in this life), creator of strangled voices, inventor of absence.

Many of his unfinished endings are unforgettable. Like that of "No-One Turned the Lights On", where he tells us he was "among the last, bumping into the furniture". An unforgettable ending. Sometimes I play at thinking no-one in my house turns the lights on. From today on, having recovered the memory of Felisberto's tales without an ending, I shall also play at being the last, bumping into the furniture. I like my lonely man's parties. They are like life itself, like any of Felisberto's stories: an unfinished party, but a real party at that.

29) I was going to write about the day I saw Salinger in New York, when my attention veered towards the nightmare I had yesterday, which assumed a curiously comical side.

They found out about my deceit in the office and sacked me. Huge drama, cold sweats, unbearable nightmare, until the comical side of the tragedy of my dismissal appeared. I made the decision not to devote more than a single line to my drama, it should not occupy any more space in my diary. Stifling my laughter, I wrote this: "I do not intend to discuss the ridiculous matter of losing my job, I am going to copy Cardinal Roncalli on the afternoon he was named head of the Catholic Church, when he noted down briefly in his diary, 'Today I was appointed Pope.' Or I shall imitate Louis XVI, not a particularly shrewd man, who on the day of the storming of the Bastille wrote in his diary, '*Rien*.'"

30) I thought that finally I was going to be able to write about Salinger when, flicking through the Culture pages of the newspaper, I suddenly came across news of a recent tribute to Pepín Bello in Huesca, his native city.

It was like receiving a visit from Pepín Bello.

The news was accompanied by a text written by Ignacio Vidal-Folch and an interview by Antón Castro with the archetypal (Spanish) writer of the No.

Vidal-Folch writes, "Having an artistic mentality and refusing to give it a free hand opens up two paths: one, a sense of frustration [. . .], another, much less common, advocated by some oriental spirits and requiring a certain refinement of the soul, is that which guides Pepín Bello's footsteps: to renounce without lamentation the expression of one's own gifts can be a spiritually aristocratic virtue and, when one yields to it without recourse to contempt for one's peers, boredom of life or indifference towards art, then it has something of the divine [. . .] I imagine Lorca, Buñuel and Dalí commenting that it was a shame that Pepín did not work, having so much talent. Bello paid no attention. Going against them like this seems to me a more considerable work of art than, for example, the amusing and ingenious drawings of artists Dalí considered to be 'putrid', which Bello helped to create."

I got up from the sofa to put on some background music by Tony Fruscella, another of my favourite artists. Then I returned to the sofa, curious to know what Pepín Bello had to say in the interview.

A few days ago Ferrer Lerín, the poet vulturologist, appeared to me while I was sitting on the sofa. Today Pepín Bello has done the same. I think this is the ideal place in my house for the ghosts of extreme negativity, the ideal place for them to make contact with me.

"José Bello Lasierra," Antón Castro begins, "is an unlikely figure. No narrator could have imagined a man like this, with his glossy skin like a *zagalejo*, broken by a snow-white moustache."

For a moment I thought about how much unlikely figures appeal to me, then I wondered what on earth a *zagalejo* might be, and the dictionary solved the mystery: "underskirt, part of regional dress".

To be honest, it did not solve the mystery at all, but made it much more complicated. And I ended up travelling so far with the underskirt that I became very receptive, immensely open to everything, to the point that, on the border of reason and dreams, I received a visit from the unlikely Pepín Bello.

When I saw him, all I could think was to ask him a question from the sofa, an incredibly simple question, because I know that he is simple, as simple (I said to myself) as afternoon tea.

"I have never met a woman as beautiful as Ava Gardner," he said to me. "Once, we spent a long time together, sitting on a sofa by a lamp. I stared at her. 'What are you looking at?' she asked me. 'What do you think? You, darling, you.' Incredible. I remember that at that moment I was staring at the whites of her eyes, which were like those old porcelain dolls, white turning blue in the cornea. She was laughing. And I told her, 'No, don't laugh. You're such a monster.'"

He fell silent and I wanted to ask him the simple question I had thought of, but realised that, however simple it may have been, I had completely forgotten it. No-one turned the lights on. Suddenly he began to leave, he disappeared down the corridor, bumping into the furniture, crying out like a newspaper seller in the street,

"Extra! Extra! I'm the Pepín Bello of the manuals and dictionaries!"

31) I saw Salinger on a bus on New York's Fifth Avenue. I saw him, I'm sure it was him. This happened three years ago when, just like now, I feigned depression and was granted sick-leave for a long period. I took the liberty of spending a weekend in New York. I did not stay longer because obviously I did not want to run the risk of being called by the office and of not being at home. I was only in New York for two and a half days, but it can hardly be said I wasted the time. Because I saw Salinger, no less. It was him, I'm sure. He was the very image of the elderly gentleman photographed not long before, pulling a shopping cart as he left a supermarket in New Hampshire.

Jerome David Salinger. There he was on the other side of the bus. He blinked occasionally. Otherwise I'd have thought he was a statue rather than a man. It was him. Jerome David Salinger, an indispensable name in any attempt to write the history of the art of the No.

Author of four books as impressive as they are famous – *The Catcher in the Rye* (1951), *Nine Stories* (1953), *Franny and Zooey* (1961) and *Raise High the Roof Beam, Carpenters and Seymour: An Introduction* (1963) – as I write, he has not published anything else, which is to say he has spent thirty-six years in strict silence, accompanied, what's more, by a legendary obsession for protecting his private life.

I saw him on the Fifth Avenue Bus. I saw him by chance, in fact I saw him because I was staring at the girl at his side, whose mouth was open in a peculiar way. The girl was reading a cosmetic advertisement in the wall panel of the bus. Apparently, when the girl read, she relaxed slightly at the jaw. In that short moment while the girl's mouth was open, lips were parted, to use one of Salinger's expressions, she was probably the most fatal girl in all Manhattan.

I fell in love. I, a poor, old, hunchbacked Spaniard, with no hope of arousing the same response, fell in love. And, though old and hunchbacked, I acted without a complex, I acted like any other man who finds himself suddenly in love, I mean the first thing I did was look to see if she was with a man. And that's when I saw Salinger and was rooted to the spot: two emotions in under five seconds.

Without expecting it, I was caught between the rush of love I felt for a stranger and the discovery, open to very few, that I was travelling with Salinger. I was caught between women and literature, between the onset of love and the possibility of talking to Salinger and craftily finding out, as a world exclusive, why he had stopped publishing books and why he was hiding from the world.

I had to choose between the girl and Salinger. Given that they were not talking and so did not seem to know one another, I realized that I did not have long to make my choice. I had to move quickly. I decided that love should always take precedence over literature, and then I planned how I could approach the girl, bow before her and say in all sincerity,

"I beg your pardon. I like you very much and I think your mouth is the most wonderful thing I've ever seen. I also think, as I stand before you, hunchbacked and old, that I could, in spite of everything, make you very happy. Gosh, how I love you. Are you free tonight?"

I was suddenly reminded of a story by Salinger, "The Heart of a Broken Story", in which someone on a bus, on seeing the girl of his dreams, planned a question almost identical to the one I had secretly formulated. And I remembered the name of the girl in Salinger's story: Shirley Lester. I decided that I would call my girl this for the time being: Shirley.

I said to myself that undoubtedly having seen Salinger on the bus had influenced me so much that I had thought of asking this girl exactly what a boy planned to ask the girl of his dreams in a story by Salinger. What a mix-up, I thought, all of this is happening to you because you fell in love with Shirley, but also because you spotted her next to the elusive Salinger.

I realised that to approach Shirley and tell her I loved her deeply and was nuts about her was a bad idea. Worse is what occurred to me afterwards. Fortunately I did not decide to put it into practice. It occurred to me to approach Salinger and say to him,

"Gosh, how I love you, Salinger. Would you mind telling me why you have not published anything in so many years? Is there an essential reason why one should stop writing?"

Fortunately I did not go up to Salinger and ask him such a thing. But I have to confess I had an even worse idea. I considered going up to Shirley and saying to her,

"Please don't misunderstand, Miss. My card. I live in Barcelona and I have a good job, though I'm off sick at the moment, which is how I've managed to travel to New York. May I telephone you this afternoon, or in the very near future, tonight for example? I hope I don't sound too desperate. I suppose I am, really."

In the end I didn't dare to go up to Shirley and say such a thing either. She would have told me to go jump in a lake, somewhat difficult, since there are not many lakes on New York's Fifth Avenue.

I then thought of using an old trick, going up to Shirley and asking her in my nearly perfect English,

"Excuse me, but aren't you Wilma Pritchard?"

To which Shirley would have replied coldly,

"No."

"That's funny," I could have gone on, "I was willing to swear you were Wilma Pritchard. Uh. You don't by any chance come from Seattle?"

"No."

Fortunately I also realised in time that I wouldn't have got anywhere with that kind of line. Women know the trick of going up to them and pretending to confuse them with some-body else by heart. They're quite familiar with the "By the way, Miss, haven't we met before?" and only make as if they're falling into the trap if they like you. That day, in the Fifth Avenue Bus, there was little chance of Shirley liking me, since I was very hunchbacked and sweaty, my hair had been flattened and was stuck to the scalp, revealing an incipient baldness, my shirt had a horrible coffee stain, and I was not feeling at all sure of myself. For a moment I thought that I stood to make a better impression on Salinger than on Shirley. I decided to go up to him and ask him,

"Mr Salinger, I am an admirer of yours, but I haven't come to ask you why you have not published in over thirty years, what interests me is your opinion regarding the day Lord Chandos perceived that the endless cosmic whole of which we are part could not be described in words. I wondered if you'd had the same notion and that's why you stopped writing."

In the end I didn't go up and ask him all of this either. He would have told me to go jump in a Fifth Avenue lake. Then again, asking him for an autograph wasn't a brilliant idea either.

"Mr Salinger, would you be so kind as to imprint your legendary signature on this scrap of paper? Gosh, how I admire you."

"I'm not Salinger," he would have answered. Not in vain had he protected his privacy with a will of iron for thirty-three years. Besides, I would have felt terribly embarrassed. Of course I could then have made the most of the situation to turn to Shirley and ask her to give me an autograph. She might have smiled and allowed me to strike up a conversation.

"The real reason I've asked for your autograph, Miss, is that I love you. I get pretty lonesome in New York and I can only think of stupid ways to try and engage with another human being. But it's very much true that I love you. It was love at first sight. Did you know that you're travelling next to the most reclusive writer in the world? My card. I am the most reclusive writer in the world, but so is the gentleman sitting next to you, who has just refused to give me his autograph."

I was desperate by now and becoming increasingly drenched in sweat in the Fifth Avenue Bus when suddenly I saw that Salinger and Shirley knew one another. He gave her a peck on the cheek while indicating that they needed to get off at the next stop. The two of them stood up together, talking quietly. Clearly Shirley was Salinger's love. Life is horrendous, I said to myself. But immediately I thought that nobody could change this and it was better not to waste time searching for adjectives to describe life. Seeing that they were making their way towards the rear exit door, I headed in the same direction. I do not like to dwell on mishaps, I always try to turn setbacks to my advantage. I told myself that, in the absence of new novels or stories by Salinger, I could read what I heard him say on the bus as a new literary instalment from the author. As I say, I know how to turn setbacks to my advantage. And I think that future readers of these notes without a text will thank me for it, since I like to imagine their delight when they discover that the pages of my note-book contain nothing less than a short unpublished text by Salinger: the words I heard him say that day.

I reached the rear exit door shortly after the couple had gone down the steps. I got off and strained my ears, with a certain amount of emotion, after all I was about to have access to unpublished material by a mythical writer.

"The key," I heard Salinger say. "It's time I had it. Give it here."

"What?" said Shirley.

"The key," Salinger repeated. "It's time I had it. Give it here."

"Oh gosh," said Shirley. "I didn't dare tell you . . . I lost it."

They paused next to a garbage bin. I stopped a few feet away and pretended to search in one of my jacket pockets for a packet of cigarettes.

Suddenly Salinger spread his arms wide and Shirley, sobbing, went towards them.

"Don't worry," he said. "For Chrissake, don't worry about it!"

They didn't move and I had to continue walking, I couldn't just stand there without saying a word and give away the fact that I was spying on them. I took a few steps, and played with the idea that I was crossing a border, a kind of ambiguous, virtually invisible line where the ends of unpublished stories are hidden. Then I looked back to see how it was all progressing. They were leaning against the bin, holding each other tighter than before, the two of them crying now. I had the impression that Salinger, in between sobs, carried on repeating what I had heard him say earlier:

"Don't worry. For Chrissake, don't worry about it!"

I left them to it, I moved away. The problem with Salinger is that he had a certain tendency to repeat himself.

32) On Christmas Day 1936, Jorge Luis Borges published an article in the magazine El hogar, to which he gave the title

"Enrique Banchs Celebrates Twenty-Five Years of Marriage to Silence".

In his article, Borges begins by saying that the poetic function – "the vehement and solitary practice of combining words that startle whoever hears them" – suffers from mysterious interruptions, mournful and arbitrary eclipses.

Borges refers to the very common case of the poet who, at times capable, at others is almost embarrassingly incompetent. But there is another, stranger case, writes Borges, which is more admirable: the case of the man who, in unlimited possession of a skill, spurns its use, opting instead for inaction, silence. And he quotes Rimbaud, who at the age of seventeen composed *Le bateau ivre* and at nineteen was as indifferent to literature as to glory, pursuing hazardous adventures in Germany, in Cyprus, in Java, in Sumatra, in Abyssinia and in the Sudan, the peculiar pleasures of syntax having been quelled in him by the pleasures of politics and trade.

Borges refers to Rimbaud by way of introduction to the case that interests him, that of the Argentinian poet Enrique Banchs, about whom he writes, "In the city of Buenos Aires, in 1911, Enrique Banchs published *La urna*, his finest work and one of the finest in Argentinian literature; then, mysteriously, he fell silent. He has remained silent for twenty-five years."

What Borges did not know on Christmas Day 1936 was that Banchs' silence would last fifty-seven years, would sail past its golden wedding anniversary.

"*La urna*," Borges tells us, "is a contemporary book, a new book. An eternal book, rather, if we dare to utter that portentous or hollow word. Its two virtues are limpidness and trembling, not scandalous invention nor experimentation

charged with the future [. . .] *La urna* has escaped the belli-
cose prestige of controversy. Enrique Banchs has been
compared to Virgil. Nothing more agreeable for a poet; also,
nothing less stimulating for his audience [. . .] A sonnet by
Banchs may give us the key to his improbable silence, where
he talks of his soul, *which, secular pupil, prefers heroic / ruins to
the now diminished palm* [. . .] It may be, as for Georges Maurice
de Guérin, that the literary profession strikes him as unreal,
in essence and in the sought-after praise. It may be that he prefers
not to weary time with his name and reputation . . ."

Borges proposes one final solution to the reader wishing
to solve the mystery of Enrique Banchs' silence: "His own
dexterity may cause him to spurn literature as a game that is
too easy."

33) Another happy sorcerer who refused to practise his
magic was the Baron of Teive, Fernando Pessoa's least
famous alter ego, his suicidal alter ego. Or, rather, his semi-
alter ego, since of him, as of Bernardo Soares, it may be said
that "while his personality is not mine, it is not different to
mine, but a simple mutilation of it".

I fell to thinking about the baron this morning, I thought
about him after the terrible awakening I had. It was a
morning of cruel, violent anguish. I woke up feeling as
though anguish were boring through my bones and flowing
up my veins until it cracked open my skin. Waking up was
horrible. To put it out of my mind as quickly as possible, I
went in search of Fernando Pessoa's *The Book of Disquiet*. I
decided that, however hard the passage I chanced on when

I opened Pessoa's anguished diary, it had to be less painful than the horrible experience of waking up. This system of visiting others' anguish in order to reduce the intensity of my own has always worked well for me.

I came across a passage which talks of dreams and, as so much of Pessoa's work, seems to have been written under the influence of brandy: "I never sleep. I live and dream or, rather, I dream in life and dream in sleep, which is also life . . ."

After Pessoa, I thought about the Baron of Teive. I suppose this is the last exception I shall make in this book of footnotes for suicide Bartlebys. I went looking for *The Education of the Stoic*, the only manuscript to have been left by this semi-alter ego of Pessoa's. The book has a subtitle which clearly points to its aristocratic author's condition as a writer of the No: *On the Impossibility of Producing Superior Art*.

The Baron of Teive writes in the preface to his brief and only book, "I sense that the end of my life is close, because I myself will it so [. . .]. To kill myself, I am going to kill myself. But I wish to leave at least an intellectual record of my life [. . .]. This will be my only manuscript [. . .]. I sense that the lucidity of my soul is giving me strength for words: not to undertake a work I would never be able to complete, but at least to explain in simple terms why I did not undertake it."

The Education of the Stoic is a strange and rather moving book. In its few pages, the baron, who was very shy and unlucky with women – as I am, to go no further – gives us his vision of the world and the books he would have written had it not been that he preferred not to write them.

The reason he did not bother to write them is to be found

in the subtitle and in statements like the following (which recalls the Bartlebyan syndrome that affected Joubert): "The dignity of intelligence lies in recognising that it is limited and that the universe exists outside it."

Given, therefore, the impossibility of producing superior art, the baron chooses to cross over, with all the dignity in the world, to the land of unhappy sorcerers who renounce the deceptive magic of a few, well-chosen words in one or two books that may be brilliant, but in the end are incapable of attaining the kind of superior art that blends with the whole universe.

If we add to this unattainable, universal aspiration what Oscar Wilde wrote about the public having an insatiable curiosity to know everything except what is worth knowing, we shall reach the conclusion that the baron was right to act according to his lucidity, was right to turn his attention to the impossibility of producing superior art, and perhaps even – given the circumstances surrounding his case – was right to kill himself. What other course of action lay open to someone like the baron who thought, for example, that not even the Greek sages deserved admiration, having always made on him a rank impression, "simple folk, nothing more"?

What else could such a terribly lucid baron do? He was right to tell his life where to get off and, for being unattainable, to tell superior art where to get off too. He sent them both packing in a way similar to Álvaro de Campos, an expert in saying that the only metaphysics in the world were chocolates, and an expert in taking the silver foil in which they were wrapped and throwing it to the ground, as previously, he said, he had thrown his own life to the ground.

So the baron killed himself. The final blow came when he discovered that even Leopardi (whom he considered the least bad of the writers he had read) was unfit for superior art. What's more, Leopardi was capable of writing statements like this: "I am shy with women, therefore God does not exist." The baron, who was also shy with women, found the statement amusing, but judged it lesser metaphysics. That even Leopardi should come out with such nonsense confirmed for him once and for all that superior art was impossible. The baron took comfort from this before he killed himself, since he thought that, if Leopardi came out with such stupid remarks, it was obvious that in art there was nothing to do except recognise a possible aristocracy of the soul. And depart. He must have thought: We are shy with women, God exists, but Christ did not have a library; we never come to anything, but at least somebody invented dignity.

34) For Hofmannsthal, aesthetic power has its roots in justice. In the name of this aesthetic requirement, according to Claudio Magris, he pursued definition in limit and contour, in line and clarity, raising the sense of form and the norm like a bulwark against the seduction of the ineffable and vague (which, however, he himself had championed in his extraordinarily precocious beginnings).

Hofmannsthal's case is one of the most unusual and controversial in the art of refusal, on account of his startling rise as a child prodigy in letters, on account of the writing crisis he later undergoes (which is reflected in his "Letter of Lord Chandos", an emblematic text in the art of refusal) and on account of his successive and prudent change of direction.

There were, therefore, in this writer three clearly defined stages. In the first, absolute, youthful genius, tainted with easy, hollow words. In the second, total crisis, since the "Letter" represents the ground zero not only of writing, but also of Hofmannsthal's own poetics; the "Letter" represents a manifesto of the passing away of the word, the shipwreck of the ego, in the convulsed and indistinct flow of things which can no longer be named or tamed by language: "My case, in short, is this: I have completely lost the ability to think or speak coherently about anything," which means that the author of the letter abandons the vocation or profession of a writer because no word seems to him to express objective reality. And a third stage, in which Hofmannsthal surmounts the crisis and, like a Rimbaud returning to writing having confirmed the word's bankruptcy, elegantly takes up literature again, which plunges him into the vortex of the acclaimed writer who must manage the standing of his public image, receive visits from men of letters, liaise with editors, travel to give conferences, travel to create, edit magazines, at the same time as his works are staged in German theatres and his prose gains in serenity, though, as Schnitzler has observed, what is apparent in this third stage is that Hofmannsthal never surpassed the unique miracle he represented with his amazing precociousness and with the subsequent explosion of depth which placed him on the verge of the most absolute silence, when the crisis that caused the "Letter" arose.

"I have no less admiration," wrote Stefan Zweig in this regard, "for the works that follow the stage of genius and the crisis embodied by the "Letter of Lord Chandos", his magnificent articles, the "Andreas" fragment and other successes he had. But on forming a more intense relationship with reality and contemporary interests, on conceiving greater ambitions, he lost something of the pure inspiration behind his first creations."

The letter which Lord Chandos supposedly sends to Sir Francis Bacon, telling him that he is not going to write any more – since "a watering can, a rake left out in the fields, a dog lying in the sun [. . .], any one of these objects, and a thousand others besides, over which the eye would normally slide with natural indifference, may suddenly, at any moment, take on for me a sublime, moving quality which I think the whole of vocabulary too poor to express" – this letter of Lord Chandos, which relates, for example, to Franz Kafka's *Conversation with the Drinker* (in which things are no longer where they should be and language no longer describes them), this letter of Lord Chandos captures the essence of the crisis of literary expression which affected the generation of Viennese writers at the end of the nineteenth century and speaks of a crisis of confidence in the basic nature of literary expression and human communication, of language understood as universal, regardless of the different languages that are spoken.

This "Letter of Lord Chandos", pinnacle of the literature of the No, casts its Bartlebyan shadow all the way down the writing of the twentieth century and counts among its most obvious successors Robert Musil's Young Törless, who, in the novel of the same name published in 1906, warns of the "second life of things, secret and elusive [. . .], a life that is not expressed in words and that nonetheless is my life"; successors like Bruno Schulz, who in *The Street of Crocodiles* (1934) talks of someone whose personality has split into various different and hostile egos; successors like the madman in *Auto-da-Fé* (1935) by Elias Canetti, who refers to the same object using a different term each time, in order not to succumb to the power of fixed, immutable definition; successors like Oswald Wiener, who in *The Betterment of Central Europe* (1969) mounted a frontal attack on literary deception, in a curious bid to destroy it, in order to go beyond the sign and come into contact again with the immediacy of life; more recent successors such as Pedro Casariego Córdoba, for whom, in *Falseare la leyenda*, feelings may be inexpressible, art may be a vapour and may evaporate in the process of turning the outer inwards; or successors like Clément Rosset, who in *Le choix des mots* (1995) says that, in the field of art, the uncreative man may claim superior strength to that of the creative man, since the latter merely possesses the power to create, while the former has the power to create and, at the same time, the power to decide not to.

35) Although the syndrome already had a long history, with the "Letter of Lord Chandos" literature lay completely exposed to its insufficiency and impossibility, drawing from this exposure – as is happening in these notes without a text – its fundamental, necessarily tragic question.

Denial, refusal, mutism, are gaps in the extreme forms in which the unease of culture presented itself.

But the extreme form par excellence appeared with the Second World War, when language suffered mutilation and Paul Celan could only dig in an illiterate wound in times of silence and destruction:

If a man
if a man came
if a man came into the world, today, with
the patriarchs' beard of
light: he could only,
if he spoke of this
time, could
only stutter, stutter
on on
only only.

36) Derain has written to me, he really has written to me,
I'm not making it up. I had abandoned all hope of his ever
doing so, but I'm very pleased.

He asks me for money – clearly the man does not lack a
sense of humour – for all the documentation he has sent for
my notes.

Dear colleague (the letter begins), I am sending you
photocopies of some literary documents that may be of
interest to you, that may be useful for your notes on
the art of refusal.

To start with, you'll find an excerpt from Paul
Valéry's *Monsieur Teste*. I know you've got Valéry, who is
absolutely essential for the subject you're dealing with,
but you may have overlooked the fragment I'm sending
you – the condensed pearl of a book, *Monsieur Teste*,
which is totally in line with what we may term the issue
of the No.

After this is a letter by John Keats, in which, among other things, he asks where the wonder is that he should say he would write no more.

I also enclose "Adieu", should you have mislaid this brief text by Rimbaud which many, myself included, consider to contain his explicit farewell to literature.

I'm also sending you a vital extract you need from *The Death of Virgil*, a novel by Hermann Broch.

After that is a statement by Georges Perec, which has nothing to do with the subject of denial or refusal, or with anything that concerns you and what you are investigating, but which I think may come as a refreshing pause after the rigidity of Broch.

Finally, I enclose something that on no account should be missing from a study of the art of refusal: "Crise de vers", a text by Mallarmé dating from 1896.

That's a thousand francs. I think my help is well worth it.

Sincerely,

Derain

37) I admit that the excerpt by Valéry that Derain has chosen for me is a condensed pearl of *Monsieur Teste*: "Monsieur Teste was not a philosopher or anything like it. He was not even a man of letters. For this reason, he thought a lot. The more one writes, the less one thinks."

*   *   *

38) A poet who was conscious of being a poet, John Keats is the author of decisive ideas about poetry, which are never set out in prologues or in books of theory but in letters to friends, most notably in the letter sent to Richard Woodhouse on 27 October 1818. In this letter, he refers to the *negative capability* of a good poet, namely a poet who is able to distance himself and remain neutral in the face of what he says, just as Shakespeare's characters do, entering into direct communion with situations and things so as to turn them into poems.

In this letter, he denies that the poet has any substance of his own, an identity, a self from which to speak with sincerity. For Keats, a good poet is more like a chameleon, who takes as much delight in conceiving a wicked character (such as Iago in *Othello*) as an angelic one (such as Imogen in *Cymbeline*).

For Keats, the poetical character "is everything and nothing – It has no character – it enjoys light and shade [. . .] What shocks the virtuous philosopher delights the chameleon poet." And that is precisely why "a poet is the most unpoetical of anything in existence, because he has no Identity – he is continually in for and filling some other body."

"The Sun," he continues telling his friend, "the Moon, the Sea, and men and women, who are creatures of impulse, are poetical, and have about them an unchangeable attribute; the poet has none, no identity – he is certainly the most unpoetical of all God's creatures."

Keats here seems to be announcing, years ahead of time, the frequently quoted "dissolution of the self". Guided by his exceptional intelligence and intuitive powers, he anticipated many things. This becomes apparent when, having discussed the poet's chameleon-like qualities, he asks his friend Woodhouse a surprising question for that period: "If then the poet has no self, and if I am a poet, where is the wonder that I should say I would write no more?"

39) "Adieu" is a brief text by Rimbaud included in *A Season in Hell*, in which the poet does indeed appear to be saying farewell to literature: "Autumn already! But why yearn for an eternal sun if we are committed to the discovery of divine light, far away from those who die at different seasons?"

A mature Rimbaud – "Autumn already!" – a mature Rimbaud at the age of nineteen bids farewell to what for him is the illusion of Christianity, to the various stages his poetry has been through, to his illuminist principles, in short to his huge ambition. And before him he glimpses a new path: "I tried to invent new flowers, new stars, new flesh, new languages. I thought I had acquired supernatural powers. Now you see! I must bury my imagination and my memories! The beautiful glory of an artist and storyteller snatched away!"

He ends with a statement that has become famous, clearly a farewell of the first order: "One must be absolutely modern. *No songs; hold on to a step that has been taken.*"

All the same, even though Derain did not send it to me, I prefer a simpler farewell to literature, much more straightforward than Rimbaud's "Adieu". It is to be found in the draft of *A Season in Hell* and reads as follows: "I can now say that art is an idiocy."

* * *

40) Keats and Rimbaud – I understand Derain wishes to imply to me – are present at the poet Virgil's final crisis in Hermann Broch's extraordinary novel. We can almost feel the same Keats who had envisaged the dissolution of the self (before it was a cliché) when Broch, halfway through *The Death of Virgil*, tells us that his dying hero had thought he had escaped from shapelessness, but shapelessness had covered him again, not imperceptibly like a flock of sheep, but immediately, tangibly almost, like the chaos of an individualisation and a dissolution that could not be contained any way either by spying or by being rigid: "The demonic chaos of every isolated voice, of every act of knowledge, of every thing [. . .] this chaos assailed him now, to this chaos he had succumbed [. . .]. Oh, each one is threatened by unruly voices and their tentacles, by the branches of voices, by branched voices which get tangled up and hold him in their grasp, growing out of control, in all directions, and twisting again, demonic in their individualisation, voices of seconds, voices of years, voices which knit together in the net of the world, in the net of ages, incomprehensible and impenetrable in the roar of their silence."

We can almost feel the same Rimbaud who, having envisaged new languages, had to bury his imagination when Virgil discovers at the end of his life that to reach the knowledge beyond all knowledge requires powers we do not have, requires a force of expression that would far surpass any earthly expression, a language that ought to be beyond the undergrowth of voices and all earthly tongues, a language that would be more than music, a language that would allow the eye to receive the cognitive whole.

Virgil here seems to be thinking about a language that

hasn't been found and that may be unattainable ("To write is to attempt to know what we would write were we to write," Marguerite Duras used to say), since we would need a life without end to retain a single, poor second of memory, a life without end to cast a single, second-long glance into the depths of the idiomatic abyss.

41) The quotation by Georges Perec that Derain has sent me as a refreshing pause after the rigidity of Broch parodies Proust and is relatively amusing. I reproduce it here: "For a long time, I went to bed in writing."

42) Mallarmé is very direct, he does not beat about the bush in "Crise de vers" when it comes to talking about the impossibility of literature: "To narrate, to teach, even to describe, presents no difficulty and, though for the exchange of thoughts it may be enough to take or deposit in silence a coin in another's hand, the elementary use of discourse serves universal reporting, in which all contemporary genres of writing participate, except literature."

43) Overwhelmed by so many black suns of literature, I sought a moment ago to recover the balance between yes and no, to find a reason to write. I ended up taking refuge in the first thing that came into my head, a fragment by the

Argentinian writer Fogwill: "I write so as not to be written. For many years I was written in my life, I acted out a story. I suppose I write in order to write others, to operate on the imagination, the revelation, the knowledge of others. Possibly on the literary behaviour of others."

Having made Fogwill's words my own – at the end of the day, in these footnotes on an invisible text, I am also commenting on the literary behaviour of others so as to be able to write and not be written – I turn off the lights in the sitting room, start down the corridor, bumping into the furniture, tell myself it won't be long before I go to bed in writing.

44) I should like to have given the reader the pleasant sensation that coming to these pages is like joining a club along the lines of Chesterton's *Club of Queer Trades*, where as one of its services Bartlebys Reunited – such would be the name of this club or queer trade – would make available to its members some of the finest stories which relate to the subject of giving up writing.

In the matter of Bartleby's syndrome, two stories are indisputable and may be said even to have founded the syndrome and its possible poetics. They are "Wakefield" by Nathaniel Hawthorne and Herman Melville's "Bartleby the Scrivener". Both stories contain a rejection (of married life in the first, and of life in general in the second) and, though neither rejection relates to literature, the protagonists' behaviour foreshadows future phantom books and other refusals to write that would soon flood the literary stage.

In this selection of texts, together with the indisputable "Wakefield" and "Bartleby" – what wouldn't I have given for these two characters to be my best friends? – three stories which I like very much need to be included, need to be made available to all members of Bartlebys Reunited. Each of them, in their own (very peculiar) way, recounts the birth of an idea – that of giving up writing – in the life of their protagonists.

The three stories are: "Travel and Don't Write It Down" by Rita Malú; "Petronius" by Marcel Schwob; and "Story of a Non-Existent Story" by Antonio Tabucchi.

45) In "Travel and Don't Write It Down" – an apocryphal story which Robert Derain in *Éclipses littéraires* attributes to Rita Malú, tracing it to the collection of stories *Sad Bengali Nights* – we are told how, one day, a foreigner travelling through India entered a small town, entered the courtyard of a house, where he saw a group of Shaivites sitting on the ground, with small cymbals in their hands, singing at a fiendishly high tempo a devilish song of charms which took possession of the foreigner's spirits in a mysterious and irresistible way.

In the courtyard there was also an extremely old man; he greeted the foreigner, who was, however, distracted by the Shaivites' chanting and reacted too late to the greeting. The music became more and more demonic. The foreigner wished the old man would look at him again. The old man was a pilgrim. The music came to an abrupt end, and the foreigner was filled with ecstasy. The old man suddenly turned his gaze on the foreigner and, shortly afterwards, walked slowly out of the courtyard. The foreigner thought he detected a special message in that gaze. He did not know what the old man had wanted to convey to him, but he was sure it was something important, essential.

The foreigner, who was a travel writer, finally understood that the old man had read his destiny and that, when he first greeted him, he had rejoiced at his future, only later, having read his entire destiny, to feel great pity for him. The foreigner then understood that the old man, by gazing at him, had been warning him that he was in grave danger and had been urging him to hoodwink his dreadful destiny by ceasing immediately to be what would bring him his future misfortune – a travel writer.

"In this legend of present-day India," so concludes Rita Malú's story, "we are told how the foreigner, as soon as he understood the import of the old man's gaze, fell into a state of total apathy with regard to literature and ceased to write travel books or any other kind of books, ceased to write at all. Just in case."

46) Marcel Schwob's story "Petronius" is found in *Imaginary Lives*. To write this book, according to Borges, who imitated and improved on it, Schwob had invented a curious method whereby the protagonists are real, but the facts may be fabulous and quite often fantastic. For Borges, the peculiar taste of *Imaginary Lives* derives from this contrast, which is highly evident in "Petronius", whose eponymous character is the same we know from our history books, but Schwob denies he was ever an arbiter of elegance in Nero's court, or the man who, unable to put up with the emperor's poetry any longer,

brought his life to an end in a marble bathtub while reciting lewd poems.

No, Schwob's Petronius is someone who was born in a privileged world, who spent his childhood believing that the air he breathed had been perfumed exclusively for his sake. This Petronius, a child who lived in the clouds, changed radically the day he met a slave called Syrus, who had worked in a circus and who started to teach him unknown things, putting him in touch with the world of barbarian gladiators and fairground quacks, with slant-eyed men who seemed to keep an eye on the vegetables and who unhooked carcasses, with curly-haired kids accompanying senators, with old gossips discussing city affairs on street corners, with lustful servants and brazen hussies, with fruit-sellers and inn-owners, with wretched poets and impudent maids, with equivocal priestesses and errant soldiers.

Petronius' look – which, according to Schwob, was cross-eyed – began to capture exactly the manners and intrigues of all this low-life. Syrus, to round off his task, at the city gates, in among the tombs, told him stories of men who were snakes and shed their skin, told him all the stories he knew of Negroes, Syrians and tavern-keepers.

One day, at the age of thirty, Petronius decided to write down the tales prompted by his incursions into his city's underworld. He filled sixteen books by his invention and, when he had finished them, he read them aloud to Syrus, who laughed like crazy and clapped the whole time. Then Syrus and Petronius came up with the plan of undertaking the adventures the latter had composed, of transferring them from parchment to reality. Petronius and Syrus dressed up and fled the city, took to roaming the paths and living out the adventures written by Petronius, who gave up writing for good as soon as he started living out the life he had previously imagined. In other words, if *Don Quixote* is about a dreamer who dares to live out his dream, Petronius' story is that of the writer who dares to live out what he has written, and for that reason ceases to write.

47) In "Story of a Non-Existent Story" (from Tabucchi's volume *The Flying Creatures of Fra Angelico*), we are told about one of those phantom books so highly valued by Bartlebys, by writers of the No.

"I have a non-existent novel whose story I wish to tell," explains the narrator. This novel was originally called *Letters to Captain Nemo* and later its title was changed to *No-One Behind the Door*. It came about in the spring of 1977, during a fortnight of rural existence and bliss in a small town near Siena.

Having finished the novel, the narrator says he sent it to an editor, who rejected it because he considered it not easily accessible and hard to decipher. So the narrator decided to keep it in a drawer to allow it to settle ("darkness and oblivion are good for stories, I think"). A few years later, the novel turns up in the narrator's hands again by chance, the discovery giving him a strange sensation, because in fact he had forgotten all about it: "It suddenly appeared in the darkness of a drawer, beneath a mass of papers, like a submarine emerging from dark depths."

The narrator sees in this almost a message (the novel also made mention of a submarine) and feels the need to add a concluding note to his old text, adjusts one or two sentences and sends it to a different editor from the one who, years before, had considered the text hard to decipher. The new editor agrees to publish it, and the narrator promises to deliver the definitive version on his return from a trip to Portugal. He takes the manuscript to an old house on the Atlantic coast, to a house called, he tells us, São José da Guia, where he lives alone, in the company of the manuscript, and at night is visited by ghosts, not his ghosts, but real ghosts.

September arrives with heavy swells, the narrator remains in the old house, remains with his manuscript, remains alone – opposite the house is a cliff – at night being visited by the ghosts, who seek to make contact and with whom at times he has impossible conversations: "these presences were eager to talk, and I would listen to their stories, trying to make sense of what were frequently dark, unconnected, angry messages; they were sad stories, most of them, I could tell this quite clearly."

The autumnal equinox arrives amid silent conversations. That day a squall descends over the sea, he hears it moaning from dawn; in the afternoon, a strong force grips his entrails; at nightfall, thick clouds gather along the horizon and communication with the ghosts is broken, perhaps because the manuscript or phantom book appears with its submarine and everything. The ocean roars unbearably, as if it were full of voices and dirges. The narrator positions himself before the cliff, taking the submarine novel with him, and tells us – in a masterly line of the Bartlebyan art of phantom books – that he delivers it to the wind, page by page.

★   ★   ★

48) Wakefield and Bartleby are two reclusive characters who are intimately linked. At the same time the first is linked, also intimately, with Walser, and the second with Kafka.

Wakefield – that man invented by Hawthorne, that husband who suddenly and without reason abandons his wife and home and for twenty years (in the next street, unbeknown to all, since they think he is dead) leads a solitary existence, stripped of meaning – is a clear forerunner of many of Walser's characters, all those splendid walking nobodies who wish to disappear, simply disappear, to hide in an anonymous unreality.

As for Bartleby, he is a clear forerunner of Kafka's characters – "Bartleby," Borges has written, "defines a genre which in around 1919 Kafka would reinvent and develop: the genre of fantasies of conduct and feeling" – and also a predecessor of Kafka himself, that reclusive writer who saw that his workplace signified life, namely his own death; that recluse "in the middle of a deserted office", that man who walked through all of Prague, resembling a bat, in his overcoat and black bowler hat.

To talk – both Wakefield and Bartleby seem to suggest – is to make a pact with the nonsense of existing. Both display a profound denial of the world. They are like that Kafkan Odradek of no fixed abode who lives on the staircase of a paterfamilias or in any other hole.

Not everyone knows, or wishes to accept, that Herman Melville, the creator of Bartleby, had dark moments more often than is desirable. Let us see what Julian Hawthorne, the son of Wakefield's creator, says about him: "There was vivid genius in this man, and he was the strangest being that ever came into our circle. Through all his wild and reckless adventures, of which a small part only got into his fascinating books, he had been unable to rid himself of a Puritan conscience [. . .]. He was restless and disposed to *dark hours*, and there is reason to suspect that there was in him a vein of insanity."

Hawthorne and Melville, unwitting founders of the dark hours of the art of the No, knew each other, they were friends, and expressed mutual admiration. Hawthorne was also a Puritan, even in his violent reaction to certain aspects of Puritanism. He was also restless. He was never one to go to church, but we know that during his years as a recluse he would approach his window and watch those making their way to church, and his look is said to have contained the brief history of the Dark Side in the art of the No. His vision was clouded by the terrible Calvinist doctrine of predestination. This is the side to Hawthorne that so fascinated Melville, who to praise him spoke of the *great power of blackness*, that nocturnal side that we find in Melville as well.

Melville was convinced that there was some secret in Hawthorne's life that had never been revealed, and which accounted for the gloomy passages in his books, and it is strange that he should think this if we bear in mind that such imaginings were equally typical of him, whose conduct was more than gloomy, particularly once he understood that, after his first, celebrated great literary successes – he was mistaken for a journalist, for a maritime reporter – he could only hope for unbroken failure as a writer.

It is odd, but so much talk of Bartleby's syndrome and I still hadn't mentioned in these footnotes that Melville had the syndrome before his character existed, which might lead us to think he may have created Bartleby in order to describe his own syndrome.

It is also odd to observe how, so many pages into this diary – which, by the way, is cutting me off from the outside world and turning me into a ghost: the days I go for a walk locally, I find myself imitating Wakefield, as though I too had a wife and she thought I was dead and I carried on living in the next street, writing this book of footnotes and spying on her from time to time, spying on her, for example, when she goes shopping – I had hardly said anything till now about literary failure as a direct cause of the appearance of the Evil One, the illness, the syndrome, the refusal to continue writing. However, the case of failures, all things considered, is not especially interesting, it's too obvious, there is no merit in being a writer of the No because you have failed. Failure throws too much light and not enough shade of mystery on the cases of those who give up writing for such a vulgar reason.

If suicide is a decision of such excessively radical complexity that in the end it becomes an incredibly simple one, to leave off writing because one has failed strikes me as even more overwhelmingly simple. However, one case of failure I'm prepared to make an exception for is that of Melville. He has the right to whatever he wants (given that he invented the simple, but at the same time extremely complex, subtle acceptance of Bartleby, a character who never opted for the thick, straight line of death by his own hand, and certainly not for tears and desertion in the face of failure; no, Bartleby, when confronted by failure, conceded magnificently, he did not commit suicide or become interminably bitter, he simply ate ginger-nuts, which was all that would allow him to carry on "preferring not to"), I forgive Melville everything.

The relative (relative because he came up with another

failure, Bartleby's, and so eased his conscience) disaster of Melville's literary career can be summed up in the following way: after his first adventure stories, which met with great success because he was mistaken for a mere chronicler of maritime life, the publication of *Mardi* completely disconcerted his public, since it was, and still is, a fairly unreadable novel, although its plot prefigures future works by Kafka: it is about an endless pursuit over an endless sea. *Moby Dick*, in 1851, alarmed virtually everyone who bothered to read it. *Pierre or the Ambiguities* displeased the critics hugely and *The Piazza Tales* (where the story "Bartleby" finally ended up, having been published anonymously three years earlier in a magazine) went unnoticed.

It was in 1853 that Melville, who was only thirty-four, reached the conclusion that he had failed. While he had been considered a chronicler of maritime life, everything had been fine, but when he began to produce masterpieces, the public and critics condemned him to failure with the absolute unanimity of mistaken occasions.

In 1853, in view of his failure, he wrote "Bartleby the Scrivener", a story containing the antidote to his depression and the seed of his future movements, which, three years later, would give rise to *The Confidence-Man*, the story of a very special trickster (who in time would come to be associated with Duchamp) and a stunning catalogue of rough, sombre images, which appeared in April 1857 and would be the last prose work he published.

Melville died in 1891, forgotten. During his final thirty-four years he wrote a long poem, travel memoirs and, shortly before his death, the novel *Billy Budd*, another masterpiece – the pre-Kafkan story of a trial: the story of a sailor unfairly sentenced to death, sentenced as if he had to expiate the sin of having been young, brilliant and innocent – a masterpiece that would not be published until thirty-three years after his death.

Everything he wrote in the last thirty-four years of his life was done à la Bartleby, at a slow pace, as if he preferred not to, and in a clear act of rejecting the world that had rejected him. When I think of this act of rejection of his, I remember something Maurice Blanchot said about all those who knew, at the right time, how to reject the pleasant appearance of a flat, almost always empty, communication, which, it may be said, is so in vogue among today's literati: "The act of rejecting is difficult and rare, though identical in each of us from the moment we have grasped it. Why difficult? Because you have to reject not only the worst, but also a reasonable appearance, an outcome that some would call happy."

When Melville stopped searching for a happy outcome and stopped thinking about publishing, when he decided to behave in the manner of those beings who "prefer not to", he spent years searching for a job, any job, to keep his family afloat. When eventually he found one – which wasn't until 1866 – his destiny coincided with none other than that of Bartleby, his strange creature.

Parallel lives. During the final years of his life, Melville, like Bartleby, "the last column of some ruined temple", worked as a clerk in an untidy office in New York City.

Impossible not to relate the office of Bartleby's inventor to that of Kafka and what Kafka wrote to Felice Bauer, saying that literature was excluding him from life, namely from the office. If these dramatic words have always made me laugh – more so today, when I'm in a good mood and

I remember Montaigne, who remarked that our peculiar condition is that we are made as much to be laughed at as to laugh – other words addressed by Kafka to Felice Bauer, but less famous than the first, make me laugh even more. I often used to bring them to mind when I was in my office to avoid the onset of anguish: "Darling, I absolutely have to think of you wherever I am, which is why I'm writing to you at the desk of my boss, whom I'm representing at this present time."

49) In his biography of Joyce, Richard Ellmann describes the following scene, which took place when Joyce was fifty and Beckett twenty-six, and which could have come straight from the theatre of the No:

"Beckett was addicted to silences, and so was Joyce; they engaged in conversations which consisted often of silences directed towards each other, both suffused with sadness, Beckett mostly for the world, Joyce mostly for himself. Joyce sat in his habitual posture, legs crossed, toe of the upper leg under the instep of the lower; Beckett, also tall and slender, fell into the same gesture. Joyce suddenly asked some such question as, 'How could the idealist Hume write a history?' Beckett replied, 'A history of representation.'"

50) I used to spy J. V. Foix, the great Catalan poet, in his patisserie in the district of Sarrià in Barcelona. I spotted him always behind the counter, next to the till, from where the

poet appeared to be supervising the universe of cakes. When they held a conference in his honour at the university, I was among the numerous audience; I was eager to hear him speak at last, but Foix said hardly anything that day, he simply confirmed that his work was finished. I remember being intrigued – these footnotes, this book of giving up writing, may already have been taking shape in my mind. I wondered how Foix could know that his work was already finished, when one knows a thing like this. I also wondered what he was doing if he was not writing, given that he had always written. Besides, I admired him, my whole life I had been a fan of his poetry, of the lyrical language that, embracing tradition and progressing in modernity (*"m'exalta el nou, m'en-amora el vell"*, the new elates me, the old enchants me), had brought the creative capability of the Catalan language up to date. I admired him and I needed him to carry on writing verse. It saddened me to think that his work was finished and that the poet had probably decided to wait for death. Though it did not console me, an article by Pere Gimferrer in the magazine *Destino* helped me to understand. Gimferrer, in connection with the closure of Foix's work, commented, "But the same glint sparkles in his eyes, more serenely; a visionary glow, now secret in its hidden lava [. . .] In the distance is heard the dull murmur of oceans and abysses: Foix continues to dream poems at night, even though he does not write them down."

Poetry unwritten, but lived in the mind: a beautiful ending for someone who ceases to write.

★   ★   ★

51) In "The Critic as Artist", Oscar Wilde voiced an old ambition: "to do nothing at all is the most difficult thing in the world, the most difficult and the most intellectual."

In Paris, during the last two years of his life, as a result of feeling morally annihilated, he was able to realize his old ambition to do nothing at all. During the last two years of his life Wilde did not write, he decided to give up writing for good and to discover other pleasures, to discover the wise delight of doing nothing, to devote himself to sheer laziness and absinthe. The man who once said that "work is the curse of the drinking classes" fled from literature as from the plague and took up walking, drinking and, very often, pure, unadulterated contemplation.

"While in the opinion of society," he once wrote, "contemplation is the gravest sin of which any citizen can be guilty, in the opinion of the highest culture it is the proper occupation of man [. . .]. To Plato, with his passion for wisdom, this was the noblest form of energy. To Aristotle, with his passion for knowledge, this was the noblest form of energy also [. . .]. It is to do nothing that the elect exist."

And this was how he spent his final two years. He sometimes received a visit from his loyal friend Frank Harris – his future biographer – who, astonished by Wilde's attitude of extreme laziness, would always make the same remark:

"I see you're still not doing a stroke of work . . ."

One afternoon Wilde retorted:

"Industry is the root of all ugliness, but I haven't stopped having ideas and, what's more, I'll sell you one if you like."

For £50 that afternoon he sold Harris the outline and plot of a comedy which Harris rapidly wrote and equally quickly staged, with the title *Mr and Mrs Daventry*, at London's Royalty

Theatre on 25 October 1900, scarcely a month before Wilde's death in his poky little room at the Hôtel d'Alsace in Paris.

Before and after the day the play was presented, during the last month of his life, Wilde perceived that his happiness could be extended – given the success of the production – by systematically demanding more royalties for the play showing at the Royalty, and so he proceeded to bombard Harris with all kinds of messages – for example, "You have not only stolen my play, you've also ruined it, so I want another fifty pounds" – until his death in his poky little hotel room.

When he died, a Parisian newspaper reproduced the following, appropriate words of Wilde's: "When I did not know life, I wrote; now that I know its meaning, I have nothing more to write."

This statement ties in very well with the end of Wilde's life. He died after two years of great happiness, without feeling the slightest need to write, to add anything to what he had already written. It is very likely that, when he died, he had reached the limit of the unknown and had discovered what it was exactly to do nothing and why it really was the most difficult and the most intellectual thing in the world.

Fifty years after his death, in the same streets of the Latin Quarter that he had walked down with extreme laziness in his radical abandonment of literature, there appeared on a wall a hundred yards from the Hôtel d'Alsace the first sign of life of the radical movement known as *situationism*, the first public pronouncement by a group of social agitators who in their life *drift* would shout "no" to whatever was put in front of them, and would do so guided by the same notions of helplessness and rootlessness, but also of happiness, that had moved the final threads in Wilde's existence.

This first sign of situationist life was a piece of graffiti a hundred yards from the Hôtel d'Alsace. Some have called it a tribute to Wilde. The graffiti, written by the followers of Guy Debord, who would soon propose opening the roofs of great cities to pedestrian traffic, read as follows: "*Ne travaillez jamais*" (Never work).

52) Julio Ramón Ribeyro – a Peruvian writer, Walserian in his discretion, always writing as if on tiptoe to avoid running up against his sense of shame or running up against, because it might happen, Vargas Llosa – always harboured the suspicion, which turned into conviction, that there is a series of books which form part of the history of the No, though they may not exist. These phantom books, invisible texts, are the ones that knock at our door one day and, when we go to receive them, for what is often a trivial reason, they disappear; we open the door and they are no longer there, they have gone. It was undoubtedly a great book, the great book that was inside us, the one we were really destined to write, *our book*, the very book we shall never be able to write or read now. But that book, let it be clear, exists, it is held in suspension in the history of the art of the No.

"Reading Cervantes recently," writes Ribeyro in *The Temptation of Failure*, "I experienced a light sensation that unfortunately I wasn't in time to capture (why? someone interrupted me, the phone rang, I don't know), but I remember I felt driven to start something . . . Then everything faded. We all have a book, possibly a great book, but in the tumult of our inner lives it rarely emerges or is so fleeting that we don't have time to pin it down."

53) Henry Roth was born in 1906 in a village of Galicia (which at the time belonged to the Austro-Hungarian Empire) and died in the United States in 1995. His parents emigrated to America, and he grew up as a Jewish child in New York, an experience he recounted in a wonderful novel, *Call It Sleep*, published when he was twenty-eight.

The novel passed unnoticed, and Roth decided to devote himself to other things, working in professions as varied as plumber's apprentice, nurse in a mental hospital and duck-breeder.

Thirty years later, *Call It Sleep* was republished and in a few weeks it became a classic of North American literature. Roth was astonished and reacted to his success by taking the decision to publish something else one day, with the proviso that it be well after his eightieth birthday. He got well past the age of eighty and then, thirty years after the success of the reprint of *Call It Sleep*, he published *Mercy of a Rude Stream*, which his editors, given the novel's imposing length, divided into four parts.

"I only wrote my novel," he said at the end of his days, "to rescue frayed memories glowing softly in my mind."

The novel was written "to make dying easier". In it, artistic recognition is mocked in a very entertaining way. The best pages are perhaps those where he tells us his experiences on the fringes of literature – these pages, as you would expect, take up practically the whole book – all those years when no-one knows if he wrote, but he certainly did not publish, all those years when he remained oblivious to the tributaries of the river of literature and was carried along in the rude stream of life.

54) The death of a loved one not only breeds lilacs, it also breeds poets of the No. Like Juan Ramón Jiménez. Puerto Rico, spring 1956. Juan Ramón had spent his life believing that he would die any moment. When people said, "See you tomorrow", he would reply, "Tomorrow? Where will I be tomorrow?" However, after saying goodbye in this manner when he was left alone and went to his house, he would remain calm and start looking at his papers and things. His friends said that he fluctuated between the idea that he could die like his father in his sleep – he had been shaken from his sleep to receive the news – and the idea that physically there was nothing wrong with him. He described this aspect of his personality as "aristocracy in adversity".

He had spent his life believing that he would die any moment, but it never occurred to him that the first to die might be Zenobia, his wife, his lover, his companion, his secretary, his hands for everything practical (she has even been called "his barber"), his chauffeur, his soul.

Puerto Rico, spring 1956. Zenobia returns from Boston to die at Juan Ramón's side. She has struggled bravely against cancer for two years, but she has received excessive radiation treatment and her womb has been burnt. Her arrival in San Juan, though she does not know it, coincides with that of some Swedish journalists who are aware that the Nobel prize for that year is to be awarded to the Spanish poet. The New York correspondent of a Swedish newspaper asks Stockholm to award the prize early so that Zenobia might be informed before she dies. But when she finds out, she can no longer speak. She hums a lullaby – it has been said her voice recalled the faint crackle of paper – and the following day she dies.

Juan Ramón, Nobel laureate, is left an invalid. The lullaby has bored a hole in his aristocracy in adversity. When he is taken home after the funeral, the maidservant – who is still alive, she is over ninety, and remembers it all perfectly, she is happy to tell anyone in San Juan who wants to know – will witness a deranged reaction, Juan Ramón on the verge of converting to the art of the No.

All Zenobia's careful work ordering her husband's papers, all her work of many years, all the impressive, patient labour of a lover faithful till death, comes to nothing when Juan Ramón in his desperation crumples everything up and throws it to the ground and stamps on it in a fury. With Zenobia dead, his work no longer interests him at all. From that day, he will fall into an absolute literary silence and never write again. The sole purpose of his life will be to trample his own work underfoot, like a wounded animal. The sole purpose of his life will be to tell the world that writing only interested him because Zenobia was alive. Now that she is dead, everything is dead. Not another line, only animal silence in the background. And behind this, an unforgettable statement by Juan Ramón – I don't know when he said it, but what is certain is that he said it – for the history of the No: "My finest work is to have repented of my work."

*   *   *

55) Do you remember what Odradek's laugh was like, the most objective object Kafka included in his work? Odradek's laugh was like "the rustle of fallen leaves". And do you remember what Kafka's laugh was like? Gustav Janouch, in his book of conversations with the Prague writer, tells us that he laughed "softly in that particular way of his, which recalled the faint crackle of paper".

I cannot linger now in a comparison of Zenobia's lullaby with Kafka's or his creature Odradek's laugh because something has just urgently summoned my attention, and it is the warning Kafka gives Felice Bauer that, were he to marry her, he could turn into an artist dominated by the negative impulse, into a dog, to be more exact, into an animal condemned eternally to mutism: "My real fear is that I'll never be able to possess you. That the best I'll manage is, like an unconsciously faithful dog, to kiss your hand which, absent-mindedly, you'll have left where I can reach it, and this will not represent a token of my love, rather a sign of the desperation of an animal *eternally condemned to mutism* and to distance."

Kafka always succeeds in surprising me. Today, on this first Sunday in August, a damp and silent Sunday, Kafka has again succeeded in unsettling me and has very urgently demanded my attention by suggesting in his text that through marriage one is condemned to mutism, to swell the ranks of the No and, what is most striking, to be a dog.

I had to leave off my diary just now because I suffered a severe headache, what Valéry would call a *mal de Teste*. No doubt this headache was as a result of the *exercise in attention* to which Kafka subjected me with his unexpected theory concerning the art of the No.

It is worth remembering here that Valéry indicated that the *mal de Teste* is related in a very complex way to the intellectual faculty of attention. This is really a remarkable intuition.

The exercise in attention which led me to evoke the figure of a dog may have had something to do with my *mal de Teste*. Having recovered from it, I think about my past pain and tell myself that it is a very pleasant sensation when the ache goes away, since then one re-experiences the day when, for the first time, we felt alive, we were conscious of being human, born to die, but at that instant alive.

After all the time I have been captive to pain, I have not been able to stop thinking about a text by Salvador Elizondo which I read some time ago and in which the Mexican writer talks about the *mal de Teste* and that gesture, which is sometimes unconscious, of bringing one's hand to one's temple, an anodyne reflex of great pain.

With the headache gone, I searched through my records for Elizondo's old text, reread it and, with new eyes, felt that I had come across an interpretation of the *mal de Teste* that could perfectly well be applied to the history of the headache, the illness, the negative impulse of the only attractive tendency in contemporary literature. Referring to migraine, the wedge of burning metal in our head, Elizondo proposes that the pain transforms our mind into a theatre and suggests that what seems a catastrophe is in fact a dance, a delicate construction of sensibility, a special form of music or mathematics, a rite, an illumination or cure, and most of all a mystery that can only be solved with the help of the dictionary of sensations.

All of this can be applied to the appearance of the illness

in contemporary literature, for the illness is not a catastrophe, but a dance out of which new constructions of sensibility may already be arising.

56) Today is Monday. At sunrise this morning, I was reminded of Michelangelo Antonioni, who once had the idea of making a film while looking at "the evilness and great capacity for irony," he said, "of the sun".

Shortly before reaching this decision, Antonioni had been mulling over these verses (worthy of any noble branch of the art of denial) in *Autumn Journal*, a poem by Louis MacNeice, the great Belfast poet, who today is half forgotten: "Think of a number, double it, treble it, square it / And sponge it out."

Antonioni knew straight away that these verses could be turned into the heart of a dramatic but slightly humorous film. He then thought of another quote – this from *An Introduction to Mathematical Philosophy* by Bertrand Russell – which also had a certain comic tone: "The number 2 is a metaphysical entity about which we can never feel sure that it exists or that we have tracked it down."

All of this led Antonioni to think of a film that would be called *The Eclipse* and would be about a couple's feelings drying up, becoming eclipsed (as writers are, for example, when they unexpectedly abandon literature), so that all their old relationship disappears.

Since a total eclipse of the sun was imminent, he went to Florence, where he saw and filmed the phenomenon, and wrote in his diary, "The sun has gone. Suddenly, ice. A silence different from other silences. And a light distinct from any other light. After that, darkness. Black sun of our culture. Complete immobility. All I can manage to think is that during the eclipse feelings will probably dry up as well."

The day *The Eclipse* was first shown, he said that he would always be left with the doubt whether he should not have headed his film with these two verses by Dylan Thomas in *Out of the Sighs*: "There must, be praised, some certainty, / If not of loving well, then not."

It seems that for me, tracker of Bartlebys and literary eclipses, Dylan Thomas' verses are very easy to modify: "There must, be praised, some certainty, / If not of writing well, then not."

57) I remember Luis Felipe Pineda, a school friend of mine, very well, just as I remember his "archive of abandoned poems".

I shall always remember Pineda that glorious afternoon in February 1963 when, defiant and dandy, as if seeking to appoint himself the dictator of fashion and school morality, he came into class with his top button undone.

We silently hated wearing uniform and especially having to do up our top button, so a gesture as daring as this was important for everybody, most of all for me. I discovered something that would be important in my life: informality.

Yes, that daring gesture by Pineda remained for ever etched in my memory. To cap it all, not one teacher took a hand in the matter, nobody dared to reprimand Pineda, the new arrival, "the new boy" we called him, because he joined the school halfway through the year. Nobody punished him, and this confirmed what had already become an open secret: Pineda's distinguished family, with its overgenerous donations, was in very good standing with the school governors.

Pineda came into class that day – we were in Year 11 – proposing a new code of dress and discipline, and we were all amazed, myself in particular. I half fell in love after that daring gesture. I found Pineda attractive, distinguished, modern, intelligent, bold and – perhaps most importantly of all – possessed of foreign manners.

The following day, I confirmed that he was distinct in every way. I was watching him half out of the corner of my eye when I thought I observed something very special in his face, a strangely self-assured and intelligent expression: leaning over his work with attention and character, he resembled not a pupil doing his homework, but a researcher absorbed in his own problems. It also occurred to me that there was something feminine about his face. For a moment it struck me as neither masculine nor childlike, neither old nor young, but ancient, out of time, marked by other, different ages than our own.

I told myself that I had to become his shadow, to be his friend and to assume some of his distinction. One afternoon, on leaving school, I waited for all the others to disperse and, doing my best to overcome my shyness and inferiority complex (due essentially to my hump, which led all my classmates to nickname me *el geperut*, the hunchback), I went up to Pineda and said:

"Do you mind if I go along with you?"

"Not at all," he replied naturally, with composure and even, I thought, with affection.

Pineda was the only one in class who never called me *geperut* or *geperudet*, which was even worse. Before I could ask him why he showed me this courtesy, he explained it to me, suddenly saying – I shall never forget his words – in a firm and immensely self-confident tone:

"No-one deserves my respect more than someone who is physically disadvantaged."

He spoke like a grown-up, or rather much better than a grown-up, since he did it nobly and honestly. Nobody had spoken to me like this before, and I remember I was silent for a while, and so was he, until he asked out of the blue:

"What kind of music do you listen to? Are you up to date?"

He laughed, having asked this, in an unexpectedly vulgar way, as if he were a prince talking to a peasant and trying to appear like him.

"What do you mean by being up to date?" I asked him.

"Not being old-fashioned, simple as that. What about books? Do you read them?"

I could not reveal to him the truth because I would make a fool of myself; my reading was a disaster, of which I was more or less aware, as I was that I could do with a hand in this area. I could not tell him the truth about my reading because I would then have had to confess that I was searching for love and so was reading Michel Quoist's *Love* or Danny's *Diary*. As for music, it was much the same: I could not tell him that I listened mostly to Mari Trini, because I liked her lyrics: "Who at fifteen has not wanted a hug? Who has not written a poem for love?"

"I occasionally write poetry," I replied, hiding the fact that it was sometimes inspired by Mari Trini's songs.

"What kind of poetry?"

"Yesterday I wrote a poem called 'Solitude Out in the Open'."

He laughed again as if he were a prince talking to a peasant and trying to be a bit like him.

"The poems I write, I never finish them," he said. "I don't even get past the first verse. I must have written at least fifty of these abandoned poems. If you like, you can come round to my house and I'll show you them. I don't finish them, but even if I did, they would never deal with solitude, solitude is for finicky, nervous teenagers, you know. Solitude is a cliché. Come round and I'll show you what I write."

"So, why don't you finish your poems?" I asked him an hour later, in his house.

The two of us were on our own in his spacious bedroom. I still had not got over the exquisite treatment I had received from Pineda's no less exquisite parents.

There was no reply, he had gone into a daze and was staring at the closed window we would shortly open so that we could smoke.

"Why don't you finish your poems?" I asked again.

"Listen," he said, finally reacting, "you and I are gonna do something. We're gonna smoke. Do you smoke?"

"Yes," I said, lying, since I smoked about a cigarette a year.

"We're gonna smoke, and then, if you stop asking why I don't finish them, I'll show you my poems, so you can tell me what you think."

He produced cigarette-paper and tobacco from a drawer in his desk and started rolling a cigarette, followed by another. Then he opened the window, and we began to smoke in silence. Suddenly he went to the record-player and put on music by Bob Dylan, music directly imported from London, bought in the only shop in Barcelona – he told me – where they sold records from abroad. I remember very well what I saw, or thought I saw, while we were listening to Bob Dylan. Now he's completely withdrawn into himself, I remember thinking with a shudder, seeing him more absent than a few minutes earlier, his eyes closed as he concentrated on the music. I had never felt so alone and I even started thinking that this could be the theme of a new poem of mine.

The strangest part came a little later, when I saw that in fact his eyes were wide open: they were fixed, they did not see, they did not look; they were turned inwards, focusing on a remote place. I could have sworn that he was foreign in everything, more foreign than the records he listened to and more original than Bob Dylan's music, which I didn't particularly like, and I told him so.

"The trouble is you don't understand the words," he said.

"Why, do you?"

"No, but that's fine with me. That way, I can imagine what he's singing, which inspires me to write verses, the first verses of poems I never finish. Do you want to see them?"

From the same drawer that held the tobacco, he produced a blue folder with a large label, on which was written: "Archive of abandoned poems".

I can clearly remember the fifty quarto sheets on which in red ink he had written the poems he abandoned, poems that, in effect, never went beyond the first line; I can clearly remember some of those sheets with a single verse:

I love the twist of my sobriety.

It'd be fantastic to be like the rest.

I shan't say it's a toad.

All of this impressed me a lot. It seemed to me that Pineda had been prepared by his parents to triumph, he was well ahead in everything, original in everything, and, besides, he had talent to spare. I was very impressed (and wanted to be like him), but I tried to hide it and adopted a gesture almost of indifference while suggesting he would do well to bother finishing those poems. He smiled at me smugly and said to me:

"How dare you give me advice? I'd like to know what it is you read, remember you still haven't told me. I reckon you read comics, *Captain Thunder* and stuff like that. Go on, tell me the truth."

"Antonio Machado," I replied, without having read any. I only thought of the name because we were due to study him.

"Oh no!" Pineda exclaimed. "*Monotony of rain behind the glass. The schoolboys study . . .*"

He went towards the bookshelf and returned with a book by Blas de Otero, *Que trata de España*.

"Here," he said to me. "This is poetry."

I still have the book, since I did not give it back to him. It was a fundamental book in my life.

He then showed me his large collection of jazz records, almost all of them imported.

"Does jazz inspire you to write poems as well?" I asked him.

"It does. What do you bet I can write one in under a minute?"

He put on music by Chet Baker – who, from that day on, would be my favourite musician – and for a few seconds concentrated very hard, again his eyes turned inwards, on a remote place. Then, as if in a trance, he took a sheet of paper and, using a red pen, jotted down:

Jehovah buried and Satan dead.

I was enthralled. And my enthrallment would increase as the year wore on. I became, just as I had wanted, his shadow, his loyal attendant. I could not have felt greater pride in being seen as Pineda's friend. Some even stopped calling me *geperut*. Year 11 is linked to the memory of the huge influence Pineda had on me. By his side I learnt countless things, my literary and musical tastes altered. Within my intellectual limits, I even grew sophisticated. Pineda's parents half adopted me. I began to view my family as an unhappy and vulgar unit, which caused me problems: for example, my mother branding me a "ridiculous snob".

The following year, I stopped seeing Pineda. On account of my father's work, my family moved to Girona, where we spent a few years and I studied for university. On returning to Barcelona, I opted to read Philosophy and Literature, convinced that I would cross paths again with Pineda, but to my surprise he enrolled in Law. I was writing more and more poetry, fleeing from my solitude. One day, at a students' meeting, I located Pineda, and we went to celebrate in a bar in Urquinaona Square. This reunion I experienced as a great event. As in the early days of our friendship, my heart beat faster, I lived it all again as if I were enjoying a great privilege: the huge joy and good fortune of being in the company of that small genius. I had no doubt that a great future awaited him.

"Are you still writing poems of a single line?" I asked him for the sake of asking something.

Pineda laughed as he had done years before, like a prince in a medieval story coming into contact with a peasant and trying to stoop to his level. I remember how he produced cigarette-paper from his pocket and without pausing wrote a complete poem – strangely enough, I only remember the first line, certainly an impressive one: "Stupidity is not my strong point" – which shortly afterwards he made into a cigarette and calmly smoked, that is to say he smoked his own poem.

When he had finished smoking it, he looked at me, smiled and said:

"What matters is that you write it."

I thought I saw a sublime elegance in that way he had of smoking what he created.

He told me that he was studying Law because Philosophy was a degree for sissies. And, having said this, he disappeared. It was a long time (a very long time) before I saw him again, or rather I sometimes caught sight of him, but always in the company of new friends, which made it difficult to have a relationship, the marvellous intimacy we had enjoyed before. One day I found out from others that he was going to study to be a solicitor. I did not see him for many years, and bumped into him again at the end of the eighties, when I least expected it. He was married with two children, and introduced me to his wife. He had become a respectable solicitor and, after years of traipsing round towns and cities in Spain, he had landed in Barcelona, where he had just set up a practice. I thought him more attractive than ever; with his silvery temples, I thought he maintained the mark of distinction that so distinguished him from the rest of the world. Despite the intervening period, my heart started pounding in front of him. He introduced me to his wife, a horrible, fat woman, who looked like a peasant-woman straight out of Transylvania. I had yet to recover from my surprise when Solicitor Pineda offered me a cigarette, which I accepted.

"You sure it's not one of your poems?" I asked him with a conspiratorial look, and a glance in the direction of that monstrous, fat woman who had nothing to do with him.

Pineda smiled at me as before, as if he were a prince in disguise.

"I see you haven't lost any of your humour," he said. "You know I always admired you at school? You taught me one hell of a lot."

My heart seized as if gripped by a sudden combination of stupor and cold.

"My duckling always speaks very highly of you," the fat woman interjected, with crushing vulgarity. "He says you knew more about jazz than anyone in the world."

I contained myself, I even felt like crying. The duckling had to be Pineda. I pictured him every morning following her into the bathroom and waiting for her to get on the scales. I pictured him kneeling down next to her, holding pencil and paper. The piece of paper was full of dates, days of the week and figures. He would read the scale, consult the piece of paper and either nod or purse his lips.

"We'll have to meet up some time, blah-blah-blah," said Pineda, sounding like a real hick.

I could not get over my astonishment. I mentioned Blas de Otero's book to him and told him I would give it back to him and apologised for having taken thirty years to do so. I don't think he knew what I was talking about, and I was reminded of Nagel, a character in *Mysteries* by Knut Hamsun, of whom the author says that he was one of those kids who die young, during their school-days, because their soul abandons them.

"If you happen to see any of your poets," said Pineda, possibly trying to be funny, but sounding unbearably common, "please don't give any of them, not one of them, my best wishes."

He then frowned, examined his nails and finally let out an obscene, vulgar guffaw, as if faking an air of euphoria in an attempt to conceal his deep sense of disappointment. He opened his mouth so wide that I could see four teeth were missing.

58) Among those who in *Don Quixote* have given up writing is the canon of Part I, Chapter XLVIII, who confesses to having written "more than a hundred sheets" of a book of chivalry which he discontinues because he realizes, among other things, that it is not worth making the effort in order to submit himself "to the confused judgement of the unthinking masses".

But, for memorable farewells to the practice of literature, none is so beautiful and impressive as that of Cervantes. "Yesterday I received extreme unction and today I am writing this. Time is short, anxiety grows, hope fades, and yet, despite all this, I still cling to the desire to live." In these terms Cervantes expressed himself on 19 April 1616 in the dedication of *Persiles*, the last page he wrote in his life.

There is no more beautiful and emotive farewell to literature than this written by Cervantes, aware that he could not write any more.

In the preface to the reader, written a few days earlier, he had already declared his acceptance of death in terms no cynic, sceptic or disillusioned person could ever endorse: "Goodbye, thank you; goodbye, wits; goodbye, jolly friends; I am dying, and desirous to see you content soon in the other life!"

This "Goodbye" is the most moving and unforgettable ever written by somebody to take their leave of literature.

59) I think of a tiger that is as real as life itself. This tiger is the symbol of the certain danger that stalks the student of the literature of the No. Because research into writers of the No from time to time produces distrust of words, there is the risk – I tell myself now, on 3 August 1999 – of revisiting Lord Chandos' crisis when he saw that words were a law unto themselves and *could not explain life*. In fact the risk of revisiting the crisis suffered by Hofmannsthal's character may befall someone who may not even know the tormented Lord.

I think now of what happened to Borges when, preparing to tackle the writing of a poem about the tiger, he set out to search in vain for the other tiger, beyond words, to be found in the forest – in real life – and not in verse: ". . . the fatal tiger, the ill-fated jewel / Which, under the sun or the diverse moon, / Obeys in Sumatra or in Bengal / Its routine of love, of leisure and death".

Borges confronts the symbolic tiger with the true, hot-blooded tiger:

> The one which decimates the tribe of buffaloes
> And today, 3rd of August 59,
> Stretches out over the prairies a slow
> Shadow, but the mere fact of naming it
> And of speculating as to its circumstance
> Makes it a fiction of art and no living
> Creature of those that walk upon the earth.

Today, 3rd of August 99, exactly forty years after Borges wrote this poem, I think of the other tiger, the one I also search for sometimes in vain, beyond words: a way to ward off the danger, the danger without which, however, these footnotes would amount to nothing.

60) Paranoid Pérez never managed to write a single book because, each time he had an idea for one and resolved to do something about it, Saramago would write it before him. Paranoid Pérez ended up going round the bend. His case is an interesting variant of Bartleby's syndrome.

"Hey, Pérez, what happened to that book you were preparing?"

"I shan't write it now. Saramago pinched my idea again."

Paranoid Pérez is a wonderful character created by Antonio de la Mota Ruiz, a young author from Santander who has just published his first book, a volume of short stories entitled *Guía de lacónicos* (Guide to the Laconic), a work which has received little attention and which, despite being a very irregular collection of stories, I do not regret having bought and read since with it has come the surprise and fresh air of the story whose main character is Paranoid Pérez, called "He Was Always One Step Ahead and It Was Really Rather Strange", the last in the book and probably the best, though the story is a little outrageous, even imperfect; but the figure of this curious Bartleby the author has invented is not to be sneezed at, at least by me.

The story in its entirety takes place in the health centre at Cascais, in the mental hospital of this small town near Lisbon. In the opening scene we see the narrator, Ramón Ros – a young Catalan brought up in Lisbon – walking peacefully with Doctor Gama, whom he has gone to visit to consult about "intermittent psychoneurosis". Unexpectedly, Ramón Ros' attention is drawn by the sudden appearance, among the lunatics, of a very tall, imposing young man with a lively and arrogant gaze, whom the management of the centre allows to dress up as a Roman senator.

"It's best not to upset him and let him be. Poor thing! He thinks he's dressed as the character of a future novel," says Doctor Gama, a little enigmatically.

Ramón Ros asks to be introduced to the madman.

"What? You want to meet Paranoid Pérez?" the doctor asks him.

The rest of the story, the rest of "He Was Always One Step Ahead and It Was Really Rather Strange", is the accurate record Ramón Ros keeps of everything Paranoid Pérez tells him.

"At last I was about to write my first novel," Paranoid

begins, "a story I had been working hard on, which takes place in its really rather entirety in that big convent on the Sintra road, I was going to say the really rather Sintra road, when suddenly one day, in a bookshop window, to my utter bewilderment, I saw a book about the convent written by a certain Saramago, entitled *Baltasar and Blimunda*. Oh really rather dear me! . . ."

Paranoid Pérez, who is in the habit of prefixing things he says with "really rather", unravels his tale, explains how he froze, full of fears that he confirmed shortly after, when he saw that the novel by Saramago was "amazingly similar, really rather similar" to the one he had planned to write himself.

"I was stunned," Paranoid continues, "really rather stunned, unsure what to make of all this, until one day I heard someone explain that there are stories that reach us in the form of a voice, a voice which speaks inside us and which is not our own, really rather not our own. I told myself that this was the best explanation I had been able to find to understand the strange thing that had happened to me, I told myself that it was very possible that everything I had planned for my novel had been transported, in the form of an inner voice, to the mind of Mr Saramago . . ."

We learn from Paranoid Pérez that, having recovered from the crisis brought on by the strange event, he started merrily thinking about another novel and carefully planned a story whose main character would be Ricardo Reis, Fernando Pessoa's alter ego. Needless to say, Paranoid's surprise was great when, just as he was about to put pen to paper, Saramago's new novel, *The Year of the Death of Ricardo Reis*, appeared in print.

"He was always one step ahead and it was really rather strange," Paranoid declares to the narrator, referring of course to Saramago. He then relates how, when two years later *The Stone Raft* appeared, he turned into stone before Saramago's new book, since he remembered having had a dream only a few days previously and later an idea which was really rather the same as the one developed in the new book by this writer who was in the annoying habit of anticipating him in such an insistent and really rather curious way.

Paranoid's friends began to laugh at him and insist that he look for more convincing excuses to justify his not writing. His friends started calling him paranoid when he accused them of supplying information to Saramago. "I'm never going to tell you any of the plans I have to write a novel again. You then go and reveal it all to Saramago," he said. And, of course, they laughed.

One day, overcoming his shyness, Paranoid wrote a letter to Saramago in which, having enquired about the topic of his next novel, he ended by warning him that he planned to adopt serious, murderous measures should his following book take place, as the one he himself had in mind, in the city of Lisbon. When Saramago's new novel, *The History of the Siege of Lisbon*, appeared, Paranoid thought he had gone mad and, by way of protest against Saramago, he planted himself in front of his house dressed as a Roman senator. In one hand he held a placard on which he expressed his great satisfaction at having turned into a living character from Saramago's forthcoming novel. Because Paranoid, who had recently devised a story about the decline of the Roman Empire, was convinced that Saramago had pinched his idea and would write about the world of senators in that dying Rome.

Dressed as a character from Saramago's future novel, Paranoid only intended to show the world that he knew every detail of the secret novel Saramago was preparing.

"Since he won't let me write," he told some journalists who took an interest in his case, "at least he can let me be a living character from his future novel."

"I've been put in the madhouse," Paranoid remarks to Ramón Ros, "what's there to say? They don't believe me, they believe Saramago, who is more important. That's life."

Paranoid makes this remark, and the story approaches its end. Night falls, the narrator tells us. It is a unique, a splendid night, the moon placed in such a way over the arches of the garden in the health centre that one could touch it with an outstretched hand. The narrator settles down to watch the moon and lights a cigarette. The nurses come to take Paranoid away. A dog is heard barking in the distance, outside the health centre. The narrator, straying from the point, it seems to me, recalls the king of Spain who died howling at the moon.

Then Paranoid uncovers another case of Bartleby's syndrome, suffered by Saramago himself:

"Though I'm not vindictive," Paranoid concludes, "it gives me infinite pleasure to see that, since he won the Nobel Prize, he has received fourteen doctorates *honoris causa* and still has plenty more to go. This keeps him so busy he's not writing any more, he has given up literature. I am delighted to see that justice has been done at least and he has been punished . . ."

*   *   *

61) The melancholy of the writing of the No reflected in the cups of tea no less, next to the fire, in Álvaro Pombo's house in Madrid.

In the dedication of *La cuadratura del círculo*, we can read: "To Ernesto Calabuig in memory of the thousand or so quartos which we meticulously wrote, rewrote and threw into the waste-paper basket and which now, with that warm air of satisfied perpetuity, in this abruptly wintry evening in the middle of June in Madrid, are reflected in the cups of tea, next to the fire."

Suddenly the melancholy of the writing of the No was reflected in one of the glass beads in the chandelier hanging from my study ceiling, and my own melancholy helped me to see reflected there the image of the last writer, with whom sooner or later, because it has to happen, without witnesses, the small mystery of literature will disappear. Naturally, whether they like it or not, this last writer will be a writer of the No. I thought I saw them a few moments ago. Guided by the star of my own melancholy, I saw them listening to that word, the last of all, falling silent, dying along with them.

62) This morning I heard from my boss, Mr Bartolí. Goodbye, office; I have been sacked.

During the afternoon, I imitated Stendhal, who devoted himself to reading the Civil Code to polish up his style.

In the evening, I decided to have a break of sorts from my excessive, but entirely beneficial, recent enclosure. I thought that a bit of worldly life would do the trick. I took myself off to Siena, a restaurant on Muntaner Street, and took Witold

Gombrowicz's *Diary* with me. As soon as I entered, I told the waitress, if a certain AlmostWatt should call asking for me, to say that I was not there.

While waiting for the starter, I savoured some passages, with which I was already familiar, from Gombrowicz's *Diary*. I again enjoyed the one where he makes fun of Léon Bloy's *Diary*, when the French writer notes down that he was awakened in the early morning by a terrible shout that seemed to have come from the infinite: "Convinced," writes Bloy, "that it was the shout of a damned soul, I fell to my knees and began to pray fervently."

Gombrowicz finds this image of Bloy on his knees absolutely ridiculous. And he finds it even more ridiculous when he reads the entry for the following day: "Ah, now I know whose that soul was. The papers report that Alfred Jarry died yesterday, at precisely the same hour and minute as I heard that shout . . ."

The absurdities do not end here for Gombrowicz, who discovers one more to complete the list of absurdities in this idiotic sequence in Bloy's *Diary*. "And finally," Gombrowicz concludes, "there is the absurdity of Jarry who, out of spite for God, asked for a toothpick and died cleaning his teeth."

I was reading this when the starter arrived and, as I lifted my eyes from the book, I caught sight of an idiotic customer who at that instant was using a toothpick to clean his teeth. I found this extremely unpleasant, but I found what followed even worse, since I then began to notice how the women at the next table were sticking pieces of discoloured meat into their oral orifices and doing it as if it were a real sacrifice for them. How awful. To cap it all, the men, for their part, as if they had become transparent, showed the inside of their calves, despite the fact that these were stuffed in hideous trousers, they showed the inside of their calves just as they were being nourished with the help of their disgusting digestive organs.

I didn't like any of this and asked for the bill, saying I had just remembered that I had an appointment with Mr AlmostWatt and could not wait for the main course. I paid and went out into the street and, on my way home, it occurred to me that there are times when my temperament is like some climates, hot in the afternoons and cold at night.

63) Every story has a character who, for slightly obscure reasons at times, is a burden to us, it's not that we can't stand them, but we have it in for them and we do not really know why.

I must now confess that in all of the history of the No I find very few characters I dislike, and I don't dislike them very much. Now, if I had to give the name of somebody who from time to time, when I read something about them, sticks in my gullet, I would not hesitate to give the name of Wittgenstein. All because of that statement of his which has become so famous and which, since I started writing these footnotes, I have known that sooner or later I would feel obliged to comment on.

I distrust those people whom everyone agrees are intelligent. Even more so if, as occurs in Wittgenstein's case, the remark for which such an intelligent person is renowned does not strike me as precisely intelligent.

"What we cannot speak about we must pass over in

silence," wrote Wittgenstein. Clearly this remark deserves a place of honour in the history of the No, but perhaps it is a place of ridicule. Because, as Maurice Blanchot says, "Wittgenstein's far too famous and overused precept in effect indicates that, since in expressing it he has been able to impose silence on himself, to be silent we must speak. But with what kind of words?" To put it simply, he might have said that there was no need to make such a song and dance.

On the other hand, did Wittgenstein really impose silence on himself? He spoke little, but he spoke. He used a very strange metaphor when he said that, should someone ever write the ethical truths in a book, stating in clear and verifiable terms what good and evil are in an absolute sense, this book would cause all the other books to explode, blowing them to smithereens. It's as if he were wanting himself to write a book that eliminated all the rest. Blessed ambition! He has a precedent in Moses' Tables of the Law, whose lines proved incapable of conveying the greatness of their message. As Daniel A. Attala says in an article I have just read, Wittgenstein's absent book, the book he wanted to write to end all the other books that have been written, is an impossible book, the simple fact that millions of books exist shows conclusively that none contains the truth. Besides, I say to myself now, how awful if only Wittgenstein's book existed and we had to abide by its law. Given the choice, supposing that only one book could exist, I would much rather one of Rulfo's than the one which, thanks to Moses, Wittgenstein did not write.

⋆   ⋆   ⋆

64) I confess my weakness for that wonderful book that Marcel Maniere wrote a few years ago, the only book he wrote, which bears the strange title – I don't think we'll ever know why he gave it this title – *Perfumed Hell*.

It is a poisonous tract in which Maniere deceives everyone from the very beginning. The first sham appears in the first sentence of the book, when he says that he does not know how to start – he knows perfectly well how to do it – which brings him, he says, to tell us who he is (it is laughable to think that people still do not know who Marcel Maniere is and that the only thing everyone agrees on is that it is not true, as he declares in his opening sentence, that he is a writer who belongs to the OuLiPo, the *Ouvroir de Littérature Potentielle* or Workshop for Potential Literature, the movement to which Perec, Queneau and Calvino belonged among others).

"As I do not know how to start, I shall say that my name is Marcel Maniere and that I belong to the OuLiPo and that now I feel a deep sense of relief because I can move on to the second sentence, always less compromising than the first, which is always the most important in any book, since in the first, as is well known, the greatest care is never enough." Mr Maniere's first sham is a triple sham because, as I say, it is true neither that he does not know how to start nor that he belongs to the literary group he says he belongs to and, apart from this, his name is not Marcel Maniere.

After the initial triple sham, new shams take place at a dizzying rate of one per chapter. Marcel Maniere parodies the literature of the No, posing as a radical debunker of the powerful myth of writing. In the first chapter, for example, he praises the merits of non-verbal communication in relation to writing. In the second, he claims to be a fervent disciple of Wittgenstein and mercilessly attacks language, showering words with discredit, saying they have never enabled us to convey anything. In the third, he advocates silence as a supreme value. In the fourth, he extols life, which he considers far superior to paltry literature. In the fifth, he defends the theory that the word *no* is of a piece with the landscape of poetry and says it is the only word that makes sense and, as such, deserves his highest respect.

Suddenly, just when we all think he is dreaming of giving up literature for good, Maniere blots the sixth chapter with tears and confesses to us, in a way that makes us feel embarrassed for him, that in fact what he has always dreamed of is a play written by him, which, with no let-up, would contain a continuous display of his immense talent.

"Since it is impossible for me," he tells us, "due to a complete lack of talent to write this play I have dreamed of, I now offer the reader the only work I have been able to compose. It is a piece of the most absurd theatre of the absurd, a very short piece in which not a single word is mine, not one (just as in this tract which the kind reader has reached the end of). Two actors are needed to perform the play, one in the role of No and another in that of Yes. My fondest wish would be to see it one day as a curtain-raiser to *The Bald Prima Donna* in that theatre in Paris where Ionesco's work has been performed, night after night, for an eternity."

The work – which Maniere sarcastically describes as "an interlude" – does not even last four minutes and consists of a dialogue between two characters. One of them, No, we imagine to be Reverdy and the other, Yes, is Cioran. Each has only one speech and the work is finished, and so this tract draws to a close with Mr Maniere taking his leave of everybody, saying that, as with literature – at this stage it is impossible to believe a single word of his – he feels that he is heading for destruction and death.

The dialogue between No and Yes is the following:

NO: Everything that was important and simple to say has been said in the thousands of years men have been thinking and exerting themselves. Everything that was profound with regard to broadening the point of view, making it more extensive, has been said. Nowadays we have no option but to repeat. We have only a few, insignificant details waiting to be explored. The modern man has only the most thankless and least brilliant task left to him, that of filling the gaps with a hodgepodge of details.

YES: Yes? We know, we feel, that everything has been said, that there is nothing to say. But what we feel less is that this evidence gives language a strange, one might even say unsettling, statute which redeems it. Words have been saved in the end, because they have ceased to live.

The first time I read Maniere's tract, my reaction when I finished it was to think, and I carry on thinking, that for its parodic nature *Perfumed Hell* is the *Don Quixote* of the literature of the No.

65) In the theatrical galaxy of the No, *I Don't*, the last play written by the great Cuban writer Virgilio Piñera, stands out alongside Maniere's work.

In *I Don't*, a strange and until very recently unpublished piece – published in Mexico by Vuelta – Piñera introduces us to an engaged couple who decide *never* to marry.

An essential principle of Piñera's theatre was always to present what is tragic and existential by means of the comic and grotesque. In *I Don't* he carries his blackest and most subversive sense of humour to its logical conclusion: the couple's *I don't* – in obvious opposition to the overused *I do* of Christian weddings – affords them a minuscule conscience, a guilty difference.

In the copy I possess, the author of the foreword, Ernesto Hernández Busto, observes that, in a masterly piece of irony, Piñera places the protagonists of this Cuban tragedy in a performance of hubris by default: if the Greek classics conceived a divine punishment for the exaggeration of passions and the Dionysian desire for excess, in *I Don't* the main characters "overstep the mark" in the opposite direction, violate the established order from the opposite extreme to that of unbridled passion: an Apollonian asceticism is what turns them into *monsters*.

The protagonists of Piñera's play say *I don't*, they flatly reject the conventional *I do*. Emilia and Vicente practise a stubborn refusal, a minimal action which, however, is all they have that makes them different. Their refusal sets in motion the avenging mechanics of the law of *I do*, represented first by the parents, then by anonymous men and women. Gradually the family's repressive order extends until, finally, even the police intervene, carrying out a "reconstruction of events" which will result in a verdict of guilty for the engaged couple who refuse to marry. At the end, the punishment is decreed. It is a brilliant ending, fitting for a Cuban Kafka. It is a great explosion of I *don't* in its marvellous subversive aspect:

MAN: It's easy to say "I don't" now. We'll see in a month (pause). Besides, as you become more intent on your refusal, so we shall extend our visits. We'll even spend the night with you and probably, it depends on you of course, we'll end up moving into this house.

The couple, hearing these words, decide to hide.

"What do you think of our little game?" Vicente asks Emilia.

"It's enough to make your hairs stand on end," she replies.

They decide to hide in the kitchen, sit in a tight embrace on the ground, turn on the gas – and let them try to marry them if they can!

66) I've worked well, I can be pleased with what I've done. I put down the pen, because it's evening. Twilight imaginings. My wife and kids are in the next room, full of life. I have good health and enough money. God, I'm unhappy!

But what am I saying? I'm not unhappy, I haven't put down the pen, I don't have a wife and kids, or a next room, I don't have enough money, it isn't evening.

67) Derain has written to me.

I suppose he felt obliged to do so after I sent him a thousand francs and asked him to make *encore un effort* and send me some more documents for my footnotes on the No. But whether he felt more or less obliged to answer me is no excuse for doing it with such bad intentions.

Dear colleague (he says in his letter), I thank you for the one thousand francs, but I'm afraid you're going to have to send me another thousand, even if only because a few moments ago, while making the photo-copies I'm sending you with such fondness, I very nearly burnt my fingers.

First of all, I'm sending you a quotation by Franz Kafka which Gustav Janouch included in his book of conversations with the writer. As you'll see, Kafka's words merely serve to warn you how useless your patient exploration of Bartleby's syndrome may end up being. Don't complain, my friend. Don't think I wish to discourage you completely with these clairvoyant words of Kafka's. Had I wanted to crush all your research into the blessed syndrome in one swoop, I'd have sent you a much more explicit statement by Kafka, a statement that would certainly have under-mined your work for good. What's that? You'd like to know what that statement is? All right, I shall include it for you: *A writer who does not write is a monster who invites madness.*

You say the statement does not undermine you? The knowledge that you devote yourself to mad monsters does not darken your brow? All right, fair enough, we shall continue. Secondly, I'm sending you writing containing Julien Gracq's angry reaction to the ridi-culous mythologisation of Rimbaud's silence, simply to warn you about the serious problem I sense in all these notes without a text you say you're writing, a very serious problem affecting their heart. You see, I am in no doubt that your notes mythologise the theme of silence in writing, a theme that is totally overrated, as the great Gracq did not fail to notice.

I'm also sending you some passages by Schopenhauer, but I do not wish to tell you why I'm sending them to you and why it is I relate them to the vanity – in the literal sense of the term – of your notes. I wonder if you are capable (you don't know how much I enjoy giving you work) of finding out why Schopenhauer and why these passages in particular. With a bit of luck, you may even excel yourself and win the admiration of a pedant among your readers who, had you not quoted Schopenhauer, would have thought you did not know everything about the unease of culture.

After Schopenhauer is a text by Melville which seems written especially for your notes, the truth is it fits your digressions on the No like a silk glove. If with the other letter I sent you Perec as refreshment, this time I'm sending you Melville, who is sure to refresh you twice as much, something you will have earned, by the way, should you have done a thorough job on the Schopenhauer.

After the refreshing pause comes Carlo Emilio Gadda, you'll soon see why. And finally, rounding off my generous supply of documents, the extract from a poem by Derek Walcott, where you are cordially invited to understand the absurdity of wanting to imitate or eclipse masterpieces and to see that the best you could do is eclipse yourself.

Sincerely,
Derain.

*   *   *

68) Kafka's words to Janouch help me more than Derain would like, since they talk of what is happening to me as I advance in the futile search for the centre of the labyrinth of the No: "The more men progress, the further away they are from their goal. They expend their energy in vain. They think they are walking, but they are only rushing – without advancing – towards the void. That is all."

These words seem to describe what is happening to me in this diary through which I drift, sailing across the seas of the wretched confusion of Bartleby's syndrome: labyrinthine theme which lacks a centre, for there are as many writers as ways of abandoning literature, and there is no overall unity, it is not even simple to hit on a sentence that could create the illusion that I have reached the bottom of the truth hiding behind the endemic disease, the negative impulse paralysing the best minds. I only know that to express this drama I sail very well among fragments, chance finds, the sudden recollection of books, lives, texts or simply individual sentences that gradually enlarge the dimensions of the labyrinth without a centre.

I live like an explorer. The more I advance in the search for the labyrinth's centre, the further away I am from it. I am like the explorer in Kafka's *In the Penal Colony* who does not understand the meaning of the designs the officer shows him: "It's very clever, but I can't work it out."

I am like an explorer, and my austerity is that of a hermit. In the same way as Monsieur Teste, I feel that I am not made for novels; their great scenes, tirades, passions and tragic moments, far from enthusing me, "reach me like miserable outbursts, rudimentary states in which all foolishness is let loose, in which a being is simplified to the point of absurdity".

I am like an explorer who advances towards the void. That is all.

69) In his day, on the occasion of Rimbaud's centenary, Julien Gracq protested about the pages and pages given over to mythologising the poet's silence. Gracq pointed out that previously the vow of silence was tolerated or ignored; he pointed out that it was quite common for the courtier, the man of faith or the artist to abandon the century in order to die silently in a monastery or country home.

Derain believes that Gracq's words may be affecting the heart of my notes, but he is completely mistaken. Defusing the myth of silence helps my explorations to lose weight and importance, which affords me a greater joy as I continue with them. In this way I avoid a certain tension sometimes provoked by the fear of failure, while keeping my ambition intact.

Besides, I am the first to demythologise the misguided saintliness so often attributed to Rimbaud. I cannot forget that he who wrote "above all to smoke, to drink strong liquor like molten metal" (a very beautiful poetic stance) was the same mean creature who wrote from Ethiopia: "I only drink water, fifteen francs a month, everything is very expensive. I never smoke."

70) In the first of the passages by Schopenhauer Derain has sent me, it is claimed that specialists can never be

talents of the first order. I understand Derain thinks I consider myself a specialist in Bartlebys and hopes to lower my morale. "Talents of the first order," writes Schopenhauer, "will never be specialists. They view existence in its entirety as a problem to be solved, and humanity in one form or another will offer each of them new horizons. Only he who takes what is great, essential and general, as the subject of his study can claim the title of genius, and not he who spends his life clarifying the particular relationship of one thing to another."

So? Who's afraid of Schopenhauer? And who said I claim to be a specialist in Bartleby's syndrome? The passage by Schopenhauer does not offend me. Rather, I couldn't agree more with its sentiments. I am not a specialist, I am a tracker of Bartlebys.

It's the same with the second passage Derain has sent me: I am in complete agreement with the philosopher. And it gives me an opportunity to talk about a fundamental illness quite opposed to Bartleby's syndrome, but just as interesting to deal with. An illness I think Schopenhauer was a good specialist in, by the way. The illness he refers to is that distilled by bad books, those horrific books that have abounded in all ages: "Bad books are an intellectual poison that destroys the spirit. And since most people, instead of reading the best to have come out of different periods, limit themselves to reading the latest *novelties*, writers limit themselves to the current narrow circle of ideas, and the public sink ever deeper into their own mire."

* * *

71) Anyone would think Derain had spoken to Herman Melville and commissioned a text about those who say *no*, about those in the No.

I was not acquainted with this text, a letter from Melville to his friend Hawthorne. It certainly seems to have been written for these notes:

> There is the grand truth about Nathaniel Hawthorne. He says No! in thunder; but the Devil himself cannot make him say *yes*. For all men who say *yes*, lie; and all men who say *no*, – why, they are in the happy condition of judicious, unincumbered travellers in Europe; they cross the frontiers into Eternity with nothing but a carpet-bag, – that is to say, the Ego. Whereas those *yes*-gentry, they travel with heaps of baggage, and, damn them! they will never get through the Custom House.

72) Carlo Emilio Gadda started novels that very quickly took off in all directions and became endless, which led him to the paradoxical situation – for someone who was king of the never-ending story – of having to cut them short and immediately fall into deep literary silences which he had not wanted.

I would call this suffering from an inverted Bartleby's syndrome. If so many writers have invented all kinds of "Uncle Celerinos" to justify their silences, Carlo Emilio Gadda's case could not be more different, since he devoted his whole life to practising, with remarkable enthusiasm, what Italo Calvino termed "the art of multiplicity", meaning the art of writing the never-ending story, that endless story which Laurence Sterne once described in his *Tristram Shandy*: "Could a historiographer drive on his history, as a muleteer drives on his mule, – straight forward; – for instance, from *Rome* all the way to *Loretto*, without ever once turning his head aside either to the right hand or to the left, – he might venture to foretell you to an hour when he should get to his journey's end; – but the thing is, morally speaking, impossible: For, if he is a man of the least spirit, he will have fifty deviations from a straight line to make with this or that party as he goes along, which he can no ways avoid. He will have views and prospects to himself perpetually solliciting his eye, which he can no more help standing still to look at than he can fly; he will moreover have various

Accounts to reconcile:

Anecdotes to pick up:

Inscriptions to make out:

Stories to weave in:

Traditions to sift:

Personages to call upon:

Panygericks to paste up at this door:

Pasquinades at that: – All which both the man and his mule are quite exempt from. To sum up all; there are archives at every stage to be look'd into, and rolls, records, documents, and endless genealogies, which justice ever and anon calls him back to stay the reading of: – In short, there is no end of it; – for my own part, I declare I have been at it these six weeks, making all the speed I possibly could, – and am not yet born."

Carlo Levi, on the subject of the endless story of *Tristram*

Shandy, says that the clock is the first symbol of this book, because under its influence the eponymous character of Sterne's novel is conceived, and he adds, "Tristram Shandy does not want to be born because he does not want to die. All means and all weapons are valid to save himself from death and time. If the straight line is the shortest between two fatal and inevitable points, digressions will draw it out; and if those digressions become so complex, meandering, tortuous, so quick that they leave no trace, death may not find us. Time may lose its way, and we remain hidden in our changeable hide-outs."

Gadda was a writer of the No despite himself. "Everything is false, there is nobody, there is nothing," writes Beckett. And at the other end of this extreme vision, we find Gadda insisting that nothing is false and insisting also on saying that there is a great deal in the world and none of it is false, everything is real, which brings him to the depths of obsessive despair in his desire to embrace the wide world, to know and to describe everything.

If the writings of Gadda – the anti-writer of the No – are defined by the tension between rational precision and the mystery of the world as basic components of his way of seeing things, during those same years another writer, Robert Musil, like Gadda an engineer, in *The Man Without Qualities* was trying to express the same tension, but in entirely different terms, in a fluid, ironic, wonderfully controlled prose.

In any case, the disproportionate Gadda and Musil have one point in common: they both had to abandon their books because these were becoming endless, they both ended up feeling obliged, against their will, to draw their novels to a close, falling into Bartleby's syndrome, falling into a type of silence they detested: the type of silence into which, let it be said, despite the obvious differences, I am going to have to fall sooner or later, like it or not, since it would be naive of me to ignore the fact that these footnotes are beginning to look more and more like Mondrian's surfaces, full of squares which give the viewer the impression that they extend beyond the canvas and seek – of course! – to encapsulate infinity, and, if this is the way I am heading, as I think I am, I shall be forced into the paradox of eclipsing myself by a single gesture. When that happens, the reader will do well to imagine a black, vertical wrinkle between the two eyebrows of my wrath, the same wrinkle that appears in the bad-tempered and abrupt ending to Gadda's great novel, *That Awful Mess on Via Merulana*: "Such a black, vertical wrinkle between the two eyebrows of wrath, in the girl's snow-white face, *paralysed him*, caused him to think: to repent, or nearly as much."

73) In *Volcano*, Derek Walcott, who sees the glow of a cigar and the glow of a volcano at the end of a novel by Joseph Conrad, tells us he could abandon writing. Should he ever decide to do so, he will surely hold an important place in any history that talks about "those in the No", that involuntary sect.

Walcott's verses, sent to me by Derain, share a certain family resemblance with Jaime Gil de Biedma's saying that, after all, it is normal to read:

One could abandon writing
for the slow-burning signals
of the great, to be, instead,
their ideal reader, ruminative,
voracious, making the love of masterpieces
superior to attempting
to repeat or outdo them,
and be the greatest reader in the world.

74) Yesterday I went to sleep using a method similar to that of counting sheep, but more sophisticated. I started memorising, over and over, Wittgenstein's saying that everything that can be thought can be thought clearly, everything that can be put into words can be put clearly, but not everything that can be thought can be put into words.

Needless to say, these sentences bored me so much that I soon fell asleep and I found myself in a Kafkaesque scene, a long corridor, from which some rudely made doors led to the different rooms in an attic. Though it received no direct light, it was not altogether dark, because a lot of the rooms were separated from the corridor not by uniform walls of planks, but by simple wooden lattice-work which reached to the ceiling, through which some light filtered in and through which some employees could be seen writing at desks or standing next to the lattice-work, peering from the slits at the people in the corridor. I was, therefore, in my old office. And I was one of the employees watching the people in the corridor. It was no crowd, but a group of three people whom I had the impression I knew very well. I pricked up my ears and listened attentively. I heard Rimbaud say that he was tired of trafficking in slaves and would give anything to be able to return to poetry. Wittgenstein was fed up by now with his humble job as a hospital nurse. Duchamp was frustrated at not being able to paint and having to play chess every day. The three were complaining bitterly when Gombrowicz, who seemed to be twice their age, came in and told them that the only one who had nothing to regret was Duchamp, who had after all left behind something monstrous – painting – something it was advisable not only to relinquish, but also to forget it had ever existed.

"I don't understand, master," said Rimbaud. "Why is it only Duchamp who has the right to no regrets?"

"I think I've already told you," replied Gombrowicz with great smugness and pride. "Because while in poetry or in philosophy there is still a lot to do, although neither you, Rimbaud, nor you, Wittgenstein, have anything left to do, in painting there was never ever anything to do. Why not recognise, once and for all, that the paintbrush is an ineffective instrument? It's like taking on the cosmos, bursting with colours, using a simple toothbrush. No art is so poor in expression. Painting is the equivalent of giving up on everything that cannot be painted."

75) The Lima poet Emilio Adolfo Westphalen, born in 1911, developed Peruvian poetry by brilliantly combining it with the Spanish poetic tradition and creating hermetic poetry in two books which, published in 1933 and 1935, stunned their readers: *Las ínsulas extrañas* and *Abolición de la muerte*.

Following his initial onslaught, he remained in absolute poetic silence for forty-five years. As Leonardo Valencia has written, "The silence brought about by the absence, for as long as forty-five years, of new publications did not consign him to oblivion, it made him stand out, it *focused attention on him*."

At the end of these forty-five years of silence, he silently returned to poetry with poems, like my friend Pineda's, of one or two verses. Throughout these forty-five years of silence, everyone would ask him why he had stopped writing; they would ask him this on the rare occasions Westphalen let himself be seen, though he never let himself be seen completely, since in public he would always cover his face with his left hand, a nervous hand with long fingers like a pianist's, as if it hurt him to be seen in the land of the living. Throughout these forty-five years, on the rare occasions he let himself be a target, he was always asked the same question, very similar, by the way, to the question Rulfo was asked in Mexico. Always the same question and always, throughout almost half a century, while covering his face with his left hand, the same – possibly enigmatic – response:

"The time is not ripe."

76) I have re-established contact with Juan, I have spoken to him briefly on the phone. He told me he would like to have a look at my Notes of the No, as he called them. He will be my first reader, I should start getting used to the idea that I am going to be read and so must slowly restore relations with what I am going to call "outside activity", meaning that

life of shiny appearance which, when one wants to lay hold of it, proves dangerously elusive.

Just before hanging up, Juan asked me two questions, which I did not answer, telling him I preferred to reply in writing. He wanted to know what the essence of my diary is, and what scenery – it has to be real – would describe this book of footnotes best.

These footnotes cannot have an essence, neither can literature, because the essence of any text consists precisely in evading any essential classification, any assertion that establishes or claims it. As Blanchot says, the essence of literature is never here any more, it is always to be found or invented anew. So I have been working on these footnotes, searching and inventing, doing without any rules of the game that exist in literature. I have been working on these footnotes in a slightly careless or anarchic manner, in a way that reminds me sometimes of the answer the great bullfighter Belmonte gave when he was urged in an interview to talk a little about his bullfighting. "Well, I don't know!" he answered. "Honestly I don't. I don't know the rules, nor do I believe in them. I feel bullfighting and, without worrying about the rules, I go about it in my own way."

Whoever affirms literature in itself affirms nothing. Whoever looks for it is only looking for what escapes, whoever finds it only finds what is here or, which is worse, what is beyond literature. That is why, in the end, every book pursues *non-literature* as the essence of what it wants and passionately desires to discover.

As for the scenery, if it is true that every book has a real landscape that pertains to it, this diary's would be the landscape one can find in Ponta Delgada, in the Azores.

Owing to the blue light and the azaleas that separate the fields, the Azores are blue. There can be no doubt that remoteness is the enchantment of Ponta Delgada, that strange place in which I once discovered, in a book by Raul Brandão, *The Unknown Islands*, the landscape where the last words will end up when their time comes; I discovered the blue landscape which will receive the last writer and the last word of the world, which will die intimately in them: "Here die words, here ends the world I know . . ."

77) I have been fortunate, I have dealt with hardly a single writer in person. I know that they are vain, mean, scheming, egocentric, impossible. And if they are Spanish, then they are envious and fearful as well.

I am only interested in writers who hide away, and so the possibilities of my coming into contact with them are even more remote. Among those who hide away is Julien Gracq. Paradoxically, he is one of the few writers I have actually met.

On one occasion, during the time I worked in Paris, I accompanied Jérôme Garcin on a visit to this secretive writer. We went to see him in his final refuge, we went to see him in Saint-Florent-le-Vieil.

Julien Gracq is the pseudonym behind which hides Louis Poirier. The aforesaid Poirier has written about Gracq, "His wish to keep to himself, not to be disturbed, to say 'no', in short that 'leave me alone in my corner and pass by' is to be attributed to his Vendean roots."

And so it is. Two centuries after the insurrection of 1793,

Gracq gives every impression of resisting Paris as his ancestors in their lands repelled the Convention's armies.

We went to see him in his hideaway, and no sooner had we greeted him than he asked us why we had come and what we wanted to see: "Have you come to see an old man?"

Later on, less cantankerous, sweeter and sadder: "Yet again I have the impression I am the last, it is a feeling that comes with old age, and it's horrible, survival makes you bored."

Gracq, through his metaphysical and Carthusian literature, imagines unreal worlds, lives in interior landscapes and sometimes in lost worlds, in territories from the past, in the same way as Barbey d'Aurevilly, whom he admires.

Barbey lived in the distant world of his ancestors, the Chouans. "History," he wrote, "has forgotten the Chouans. It has forgotten them just as glory and even justice have forgotten them. Whereas the Vendeans, those front-line warriors, sleep, peaceful and immortal, beneath the words Napoleon said of them and, covered with such an epitaph, can wait [. . .], the Chouans, for their part, have no-one to bring them out of their obscurity."

Julien Gracq, like a good Vendean, gave us the impression he could wait. It was enough to observe him, to see him seated on the terrace of his house, to see how he watched the River Loire as it flowed past. Sitting there, his gaze fixed on the river, he was just like someone who is waiting for something or nothing. Days later, Jérôme Garcin would write, "It is not only the Loire that has flowed for ever beneath Gracq's gaze, it is history, its mythology and deeds, in the midst of which he grew up. Behind him, that heroic Vendée, battered by war; in front of him, the famous island

Batailleuse, which Gracq, the young reader of his compatriot Jules Verne, very quickly made his haunt, Crusoeing among the willows, the poplars, the reeds and the alders. On one side, Clio, the past, the castles in ruins; on the other, the chimeras, fantasies and castles in the air. Gracq, as he is exalted by his work. You have to go to Saint-Florent to experience this desire to be reincarnated."

This is what Garcin and I did, we visited the haunt of one of the most secretive writers of our time, one of the most elusive and isolated, one of the kings of Denial, why deny it? We went to see the last great French writer from before the defeat of style, from before the overwhelming publication of what we might call ephemeral literature, from before the unbridled irruption of "nutritional literature", about which Gracq spoke in his 1950 pamphlet "Literature in the Stomach", in which he attacked the impositions and tacit ground rules of the burgeoning publishing industry in the days before the circus of television.

We visited the haunt of the Boss, as he is known by some in France, of the secretive writer who at no point hid his melancholy from us as he observed the flow of the Loire in silence.

Until 1939 Gracq was a communist. "Up until that year," he told us, "I really believed we could change the world." For him, the revolution was a job and an article of faith, until he became disillusioned.

Until 1958 he was a novelist. After the publication of *A Balcony in the Forest*, he abandoned the genre ("because it requires a vital energy, a strength, a conviction I lack") and chose the fragmentary writing of the "Carnets du grand chemin" ("perhaps with them my work will simply stop, in a very opportune way," he wondered suddenly, his voice suspended). At dusk, we went to his study. Impression of entering a forbidden temple. Through the window, cars and trucks could be seen crossing the suspension bridge: Saint-Florent-le-Vieil has not escaped modern noise. Gracq then remarked, "Some afternoons this thunders more than in parts of Paris."

When we asked him what had changed most since he was a boy playing on the quayside, between the avenue of chestnuts and the paddles of the washerwomen, he replied:

"Life has gone downhill."

Later on, he spoke of solitude. It was as we were coming out of the study: "I am alone, but I don't complain. The writer has nothing to expect from others. Believe me. He only writes for himself!"

There was a moment, back on the terrace, when, observing him against the light, I thought that really he was not talking to us, he was engaged in a soliloquy. Garcin would tell me, when we left the house, that he had been under a similar impression. "Not just that," he said, "he talked to himself as a knight would without a steed."

At nightfall, when it was almost time for us to leave, Gracq talked to us about television, told us he sometimes switched it on and was left speechless when he saw the presenters of literary programmes acting as if they were selling samples of different cloths.

When it came time to say goodbye, the Boss accompanied us down the small, stone staircase leading to the exit of his house. A fragrance of lukewarm mud rose from the slumbering Loire.

"The Loire is not normally so low in January," he remarked.

We shook hands with the Boss and began to go, and there the secretive writer remained, slowly emptying himself like the river, his river.

78) Klara Whoryzek was born in Karlovy Vary on 8 January 1863, but after a few months her family went to live in Danzig (Gdansk), where she would spend her childhood and teenage years: a time of which she wrote, in *The Intimate Light*, that she only had "seven memories in the shape of seven soap-bubbles".

Klara Whoryzek arrived in Berlin at the age of twenty-one and there, together with Edvard Munch and Knut Hamsun among others, she formed part of the habitual circle of August Strindberg. In 1892 she founded Verlag Whoryzek, a publishing house that only published *The Intimate Light*, and shortly afterwards – as it was preparing to bring out *Pierrot Lunaire* by Albert Giraud – went bankrupt.

In no way was it dejection arising from the non-existent reception of her book, nor the collapse of the publishing house, that led her into a radical literary silence until the end of her days. If Klara Whoryzek stopped writing, it was because – as she commented to her friend Paul Scheerbart – "even knowing that only writing would connect me like an Ariadne's thread to my peers, I could not, however, make any of my friends read me, because the books I have envisaged during my days of literary silence are real soap-bubbles and are addressed to no-one, not even to the most intimate of my friends, so the most sensible thing I could do is what I have done: not write them."

Her death in Berlin on 16 October 1915 was due to her refusal to ingest any food in protest against the war. She was a "hunger artist" *avant la lettre*, she paved the way for the insect Gregor Samsa (who with a human's will starved himself to death) and she followed the example, possibly also without knowing it, of Bartleby, who died in the foetal position, wasted on the turf of a yard, his eyes dim and open, but otherwise profoundly sleeping under the gaze of a grub-man asking if he was not going to dine today either.

79) Much more secretive than either Gracq or Salinger is the New Yorker Thomas Pynchon, a writer about whom all we know is that he was born on Long Island in 1937, earned a BA Degree in English from Cornell University in 1958 and worked as a technical writer for Boeing. After that, absolutely nothing. Not even a photograph, except for one from his school days, which shows a frankly ugly teenager and which there is no reason to suppose is Pynchon; it is probably a smokescreen.

José Antonio Gurpegui relates an anecdote that he heard years ago from his dear friend Peter Messent, Professor of Modern American Literature at the University of Nottingham. Messent did his thesis on Pynchon and, as is normal, became obsessed with the idea of meeting the writer he had studied so much. After not a few setbacks, he obtained a brief interview in New York with the dazzling author of *The Crying of Lot 49*. The years went by, and Messent, now the prestigious Professor Messent, author of an important book on Hemingway, was invited to a gathering of

Pynchon's close friends in Los Angeles. To his surprise, the Pynchon he met in Los Angeles was absolutely not the same person he had interviewed years before in New York, but, just like the other, was perfectly acquainted with even the most insignificant details of his work. At the end of the gathering, Messent dared to expose the duplicity of characters, to which Pynchon, or whoever it was, replied without the slightest concern,

"In which case you'll have to decide who the real one is."

80) Among the anti-Bartlebyan writers, the senseless energy of Georges Simenon, the most prolific author ever in the French language, stands out. From 1919 to 1980, he published 190 novels under different pseudonyms, 193 under his name, 25 autobiographical works and more than a thousand stories, not counting journalistic work and a large number of volumes of dictations and unpublished material. In the year 1929, his anti-Bartlebyan behaviour borders on provocation: he wrote 41 novels.

"I would start very early in the morning," Simenon once explained, "normally about six, and finish at the end of the afternoon; this represented two bottles and eighty pages [. . .] I would work very fast, sometimes managing to write eight stories in a day."

Verging on anti-Bartlebyan insolence, Simenon spoke once about how he slowly acquired a method or technique when producing work, a personal method which, once acquired, permits any number of ways in which one's corpus can increase without the slightest shadow of an I would *prefer not to ever appearing*: "When I started, it would take me twelve days to write a novel, whether or not it was a Maigret; making an effort to condense more, to eliminate from my style any kind of frills or unnecessary detail, I gradually went from eleven days to ten, and then to nine. And now, for the first time, I have reached the goal of seven."

Disconcerting though Simenon's case is, even more so is that of Paul Valéry, a writer who was very close to the Bartlebyan sensibility – above all in *Monsieur Teste*, as we have already seen – and yet who left us the 29,000 pages of his *Cahiers*.

But, disconcerting though this is, I have learnt no longer to be surprised. When something baffles me, I resort to a very simple trick that calms my nerves. I simply think of Jack London, who, despite being riddled with alcohol, was an advocate of prohibition in the States. It is good for the Bartlebyan sensibility to have seen it all before.

81) Giorgio Agamben – grouped with "those in the No" on account of his book *Bartleby o della contingenza* (Macerata, 1993) – thinks we are becoming poor and notably in *Idea della prosa* (Milan, 1985) makes this clear-sighted diagnosis: "It is curious to observe how a handful of philosophical and literary works, written between 1915 and 1930, still hold the keys to the sensibility of the period, and the last convincing description of our spiritual health and of our feelings is now over fifty years old."

On the same subject, my friend Juan gives the following explanation of his theory that after Musil (and Felisberto

Hernández) there is not much to choose from: "One of the more general differences that can be drawn between novelists before and after the Second World War is that those before 1945 tended to possess a culture which informed and shaped their novels, whereas those after this date, tend to exhibit a total disinterest in their cultural heritage, except in the literary process (which is one and the same)."

In a text by the Portuguese António Guerreiro – which is where I came across the quote by Agamben – the question is put whether it is possible today to talk of commitment in literature. With what and to what do writers commit themselves?

We also find this question, for example, in Handke's *My Year in the No-Man's-Bay*. What is one to write about, and what not? Can the constant dislocation between the naming word and the named object be sustained? When is neither too soon nor too late? Has everything been written?

In *Compulsive Reading*, Félix de Azúa seems to suggest that only from the strongest negativity, while believing (or hoping) that the literary word's potential is not yet exhausted, will we be able to wake from the current bad dream, from the bad dream in the no-man's-bay.

Guerreiro seems to say something similar when he maintains that the only path still open to genuine literary creation is to be tracked down in suspicion, in *denial*, the writer's bad conscience, forged in the works of the authors of the constellation Bartleby – Hofmannsthal, Walser, Kafka, Musil, Beckett, Celan . . .

Since all hope of an expressible totality has been lost, we have to reinvent our own modes of expression. I am writing this while listening to music by Chet Baker; it's half past eleven at night on 7 August 1999, the day has been especially hot and sultry. It is almost time to sleep, I hope, so I shall start drawing to a conclusion, and I shall do so in the confidence that there may yet be dark tunnels ahead, but the tracking down of the only path still open to us (opened by Bartleby & Co. in their negativity) may lead us to a serenity which one day the world will deserve: the serenity of knowing that, in Pessoa's words, the only mystery is that there's someone thinking about the mystery.

82) There are those who have given up writing for good because they believed they were immortal.

This is the case of Guy de Maupassant, born in 1850 at Château de Miromesnil in Normandy. His mother, the ambitious Laure de Maupassant, was determined to have an illustrious man in the family, and so she entrusted her son to a technician of literary greatness, she entrusted him to Flaubert. Her son would be known, and this is still true today, as "a great writer".

Flaubert educated the young Guy, who did not start writing until he was thirty, by which time he was sufficiently prepared to be an immortal writer. He certainly had a good master. Flaubert was an unbeatable master, but, as is well known, a great master does not ensure that the disciple turns out satisfactorily. Maupassant's ambitious mother was aware of this and feared that, despite the great master, everything would work out badly. This was not the case. Maupassant began to write and immediately showed himself to be a wonderful narrator. His stories reveal extraordinary powers of observation, a magnificent ability to portray characters and settings, as well as a highly personal style, despite Flaubert's influence.

In a short time, Maupassant becomes a great literary figure and lives luxuriously from it. He is acclaimed by everybody except for the Académie, whose plans do not include consecrating Maupassant as immortel. This foolishness on the part of the Académie is nothing new; Balzac, Flaubert and Zola have also been excluded from it. But Maupassant, as ambitious as his mother, does not resign himself to not being immortal and looks for a natural compensation for the academicians' indolence. He will find it in a spiral of conceit that will lead him to believe that, to all intents and purposes, he is immortal.

One night, having dined with his mother in Cannes, he returns home and performs a somewhat risky experiment: he wishes to be sure that he is immortal. His butler, the loyal Tassart, is rudely awoken by a blast that makes the whole house rumble.

Maupassant, standing before the bed, is very happy to be able to relate to his butler, who bursts into his bedroom in a nightcap and holding up his drawers, the extraordinary thing that has befallen him.

"I am invulnerable, I am immortal," shouts Maupassant. "I have just shot myself in the head with a pistol and am unharmed. You don't believe me? Watch!"

Maupassant again puts the barrel to his temple and presses the trigger; such an explosion could have brought down the walls, but the "immortal" Maupassant remains standing and smiling before the bed.

"Do you believe me now? Nothing can do anything to me

any more. I could cut my throat, and I tell you the blood would not flow."

Maupassant does not know it yet, but he is never going to write again.

Of all the descriptions of this "immortal scene", that by Alberto Savinio in *Maupassant and "the Other"* is the most brilliant, due to its inspired balance between humour and tragedy.

"Maupassant," writes Savinio, "without thinking twice moves from theory to practice, picks up a metal letter opener in the shape of a dagger from the table, stabs his throat in a demonstration of invulnerability to the knife as well; but the experiment deceives him: the blood gushes out, pours down in waves, soaking the collar of his shirt, his tie, his waistcoat."

From that day and until the day of his death (which would not be long coming), Maupassant did not write again, he only read newspapers in which it was reported that "Maupassant has gone mad". Every morning, along with his coffee, the loyal Tassart would bring him newspapers in which he saw his photograph and underneath commentaries like this: "The madness of the immortal M. Guy de Maupassant continues."

Maupassant does not write again, which is not to say he is not entertained and things do not happen to him that he could write about, but that he no longer intends to bother doing so, his work is finished, he is immortal already. However, things happen to him that are worth telling. One day, for example, he stares at the ground and sees a swarm of insects squirting jets of morphine into the distance. Another day, he pesters poor Tassart about writing to Pope Leo XIII.

"Is *Monsieur* going to write again?" Tassart asks in a panic.

"No," Maupassant replies. "It will be you who write to the Pope in Rome."

Maupassant would like to propose to Leo XIII the construction of luxury tombs for immortals like him: tombs inside which a current of water, either hot or cold, would wash and preserve the bodies.

Towards the end of his days, he crawls around his room and licks – as if he were writing – the walls. And one day, finally, he calls Tassart and asks to be brought a straitjacket. "He asked to be given a straitjacket," writes Savinio, "as you would ask a waiter for a beer."

83) Marianne Jung, who was born in November 1784 and was the daughter of a family of actors of obscure origins, is the most attractive secret writer in the history of the No.

As a girl, she played the part of an extra – a dancer, a character singing in the chorus or performing dance steps, dressed as a harlequin, while coming out of a huge egg which moved over the stage. When she was sixteen, a man bought her. The banker and senator Willemer saw her in Frankfurt and took her home with him, having paid her mother 200 gold florins and an annuity. The senator played Pygmalion, and Marianne learnt good manners, French, Latin, Italian, drawing and singing. They had been living together for fourteen years, and the senator was seriously considering marrying her, when Goethe appeared, who was sixty-five and was in one of his most creative periods, was writing the poems in *West-Eastern Divan*, a response to the

Persian lyric poems of Hafiz. In a poem in the *Divan*, the very beautiful Suleika appears and says that everything is eternal in the eyes of God and that this divine life can be loved, for a moment, in itself, in its tender and fleeting beauty. Suleika says this in Goethe's immortal verses. But in fact what Suleika says was written not by Goethe, but by Marianne.

In *Danube*, Claudio Magris says, "The *Divan*, and the superb love dialogue which it contains, bears the name of Goethe. But Marianne is not only the woman loved and sung in the poems; she is also the author of a number of the most truly sublime lyrics in the entire *Divan*. Goethe incorporated them and published them in the collection under his own name. It was only in 1869, many years after the death of the poet and nine after that of Suleika, that the philologist Hermann Grimm made public the fact that this woman had written those few sublime lyrics in the *Divan*, for to him Marianne had confided the secret and shown the correspondence with Goethe, which she had preserved in faithful secrecy."

So, in the *Divan*, Marianne Jung wrote a very few poems, which belong to the masterpieces of world lyric poetry, and then did not write again – ever – she preferred to keep silent.

She is the most secret female writer of the No. "Once in my life," she said many years after having written those verses, "I was aware of feeling something noble, of being able to say things which were both sweet and heartfelt, but time has not so much destroyed them, as blotted them out."

Magris remarks that possibly Marianne Jung realised that poetry only made sense if it arose from a total experience like the one she had lived and, once that moment of grace had passed, so had the poetry.

84) Much more than Gracq and Salinger and Pynchon, the man who called himself B. Traven was the genuine expression of what we know as "a secretive writer".

Much more than Gracq, Salinger and Pynchon put together. Because B. Traven's case is replete with exceptional nuances. To start with, we do not know where he was born, nor did he ever want to shed light on the matter. To some, the man who said he was called B. Traven was a North American novelist born in Chicago. To others, he was Otto Feige, a German writer who apparently had problems with the law because of his anarchist views. Others claimed he was really Maurice Rathenau, son of the founder of AEG, and there were even those who stated he was Kaiser Wilhelm II's son.

Although he gave his first interview in 1966, the author of novels such as *The Treasure of the Sierra Madre* or *The Bridge in the Jungle* insisted on the right to the secret of his private life, and so his identity continues to be a mystery.

"Traven's story is the story of his denial," Alejandro Gándara has written in his foreword to *The Bridge in the Jungle*. In effect, it is a story for which we do not have facts and they can't be had, which is the only fact. Denying all past, he denied all present, meaning all presence. Traven never existed, not even for his contemporaries. He is a very peculiar writer of the No, and there is something very tragic in the force with which he rejected the invention of his identity.

"This secretive writer," Walter Rehmer has said, "reflects in his absent identity all the tragic conscience of modern literature, the conscience of a writing that, once its insufficiency and impossibility have been exposed, turns this exposure into its fundamental question."

These words of Walter Rehmer's – I have just realised – could also reflect my efforts in this book of notes without a text. Of them it could also be said that they bring together all or at least part of the conscience of a writing that, once its impossibility has been exposed, turns this exposure into its fundamental question.

In short I think Rehmer's sentences are to the point, but, if Traven had read them, first of all he would have been amazed, and then he would have burst out laughing. In fact I am on the verge of reacting in the same way. Besides, I hate Rehmer's essays for their solemnity.

To go back to Traven: the first time I heard his name was in Puerto Vallarta, Mexico, in a bar on the outskirts of the city. This was some years ago, when I made use of my savings to travel abroad in August. I heard Traven's name in that bar. I had just arrived from Puerto Escondido or Hidden Port, a town that, owing to its unusual name, would have been the perfect place to hear about the most hidden writer of them all. But it wasn't there, it was in Puerto Vallarta where I heard Traven's story for the first time.

The bar in Puerto Vallarta was a few miles from the house where John Huston – who made a film of *The Treasure of the Sierra Madre* – spent the last years of his life locked away in Las Caletas, an estate facing the sea, with the jungle behind it, a kind of port for the jungle invariably battered by the hurricanes in the gulf.

In his book of memoirs, Huston describes how he wrote the script of *The Treasure of the Sierra Madre* and sent a copy to Traven, who responded with twenty pages full of detailed suggestions concerning set construction, lighting and so forth.

Huston was anxious to meet the mysterious writer, who at that time was already famous for concealing his real name: "I secured," writes Huston, "a tentative promise from him to meet with me at the Hotel Bamer in Mexico City, made the trip down and waited. He didn't show up. One morning almost a week after my arrival I woke shortly after daybreak to discover a man standing at the foot of my bed. He took out a card which read: 'Hal Croves. Translator, Acapulco and San Antonio'."

Then this man produced a letter from Traven, which Huston read while still in bed. In the letter, Traven said he was ill and had not been able to make the rendezvous, but Hal Croves was his great friend and knew as much about Traven's work as he himself did, and so was authorised to answer any questions Huston might have.

Sure enough, Croves, who said he was Traven's agent, knew everything about Traven's work. Croves spent two weeks on the film-set, collaborating actively. He was an odd and cordial man, whose conversation was agreeable (and sometimes became endless, resembling one of Carlo Emilio Gadda's novels), though at the moment of truth his favourite topics were human pain and horror. When he left the set, Huston and his assistants began to put two and two together and realised that the agent was an impostor, the agent very probably was Traven himself.

When the film opened, the mystery of B. Traven's identity

fueled speculation. It was even said that a group of Honduran writers was behind the name. To Huston, Croves was undoubtedly of European origin, German or Austrian; the strange thing was that his novels recounted the experiences of an American in Western Europe, at sea and in Mexico, and were experiences that had clearly been lived.

The mystery of Traven's identity fueled so much speculation that a Mexican magazine sent two reporters to shadow Croves in an attempt to ascertain who Traven's agent really was. They found him keeping a small store on the edge of the jungle near Acapulco. They watched the store until they spotted Croves leaving to go into town. They then broke down the door and rifled his desk, where they found several manuscripts by Traven and evidence that Croves was using another name: Traven Torsvan.

Further investigative reporting revealed that he had a fourth name: Ret Marut, an anarchist writer who had disappeared from Germany in 1922. In 1923 Traven appeared in Mexico, so the dates fitted. Croves died in 1969, some years after marrying his assistant, Rosa Elena Lujan. A month after his death, his widow confirmed that B. Traven had been Ret Marut.

An elusive writer if ever there was one, Traven used an unbelievable variety of names, in fiction and in reality, to keep his own secret: Traven Torsvan, Arnolds, Traves Torsvan, Barker, Traven Torsvan Torsvan, Berick Traven, Traven Torsvan Croves, B. T. Torsvan, Ret Marut, Rex Marut, Robert Marut, Traven Robert Marut, Fred Maruth, Fred Mareth, Red Marut, Richard Maurhut, Albert Otto Max Wienecke, Adolf Rudolph Feige Kraus, Martinez, Fred Gaudet, Artum, Lainger, Goetz Ohly, Anton Räderscheidt, Robert Bek-Gran,

Hugo Kronthal, Wilhelm Scheider, Heinrich Otto Becker and Otto Torsvan.

One of those who tried to write his biography, Jonah Raskin, almost went mad in the process. From the start he counted on the collaboration of Rosa Elena Lujan, but he soon began to understand that the widow was not entirely sure who the hell Traven was either. A stepdaughter of his managed to confuse him utterly when she claimed she remembered seeing her father talking to Mr Hal Croves.

Jonah Raskin finally abandoned the idea of a biography and ended up writing the story of his futile search for Traven's real name, a wild-goose chase. Raskin chose to abandon his research when he realised his mental health was at stake: he had started dressing like Traven, wearing his glasses, calling himself Hal Croves . . .

B. Traven, the most secretive of the secret writers, reminds me of the central character in Chesterton's *The Man Who Was Thursday*. This novel talks of a huge and dangerous conspiracy consisting in fact of one man who, as Borges says, deceives everybody "with the aid of beards, masks and pseudonyms".

85) Traven hid, I am going to hide, the sun will hide tomorrow, it's the last total eclipse of the millennium. Already my voice is growing distant as it prepares to say it is going, going to try other places. I have only existed, the voice says, if talk of me can be talk of life. It says it is eclipsing itself, it is going, to end here would be perfect, but it wonders if this is desirable. And it answers itself that it is, that to

finish here would be marvellous, perfect, whoever it is, wherever it is.

86) At the end of his days, Tolstoy considered literature to be a curse and turned it into the most obsessive object of his hatred. Then he gave up writing, because he said that writing was more responsible than anything for his moral defeat.

One night, in his diary, he wrote the last sentence of his life, a sentence he did not manage to finish: "*Fais ce que dois, advienne que pourra*" (Do your duty, come what may). It is a French proverb that Tolstoy was very keen on. The sentence ended up looking like this:

Fais ce que dois, adv . . .

In the cold darkness before dawn on 28 October 1910, Tolstoy, who was eighty-two years old and was at that time the most famous writer in the world, slipped out of his ancestral home in Yasnaya Poliana and undertook his final journey. He had renounced writing for good and, with the strange gesture of his escape, announced the modern belief that all literature is the denial of itself.

Ten days after his disappearance, he died in the stationmaster's house at Astapovo, a village few Russians had heard of. His escape came to an abrupt halt in this remote and sad place, where he was forced to alight from a train that was heading south. Exposure to the cold in the third-class carriage on the train, without heating, full of smoke and drafts, meant he contracted pneumonia.

He left behind his abandoned home and in his diary – also abandoned after sixty-three faithful years – the last sentence of his life, an abrupt sentence which, Bartleby-like, has petered out:

Fais ce que dois, adv . . .

Many years later, Beckett would say even words abandon us and that's all there is to it.

Appearing in Bartleby & Co.

NEW DIRECTIONS AUTHORS

GUILLAUME APOLLINAIRE
Selected Writings

SAMUEL BECKETT
James Joyce /Finnegans Wake: A Symposium

HONORÉ DE BALZAC
Colonel Chabert

CHARLES BAUDELAIRE
Flowers of Evil, Paris Spleen, Selected Flowers of Evil

JORGE LUIS BORGES
Everything & Nothing, Labyrinths, Seven Nights

RONALD FIRBANK
Caprice, Five Novels, Three More Novels

GUSTAVE FLAUBERT
Dictionary of Accepted Ideas, A Simple Heart

GOETHE
Faust, Part I

KNUT HAMSUN
Dreamers

FELISBERTO HERNÁNDEZ
Lands of Memory

JAMES JOYCE
James Joyce /Finnegans Wake: A Symposium, Stephen Hero

FRANZ KAFKA
Amerika